Erotic Short Sex Stories

A Collection Of BDSM, Hard Sex and Virgin Stories

Violetee Pink

Erotic Short Sex Stories

© Copyright 2021 Violetee Pink - All rights reserved.

The content contained within this book may not be reproduced, duplicated or transmitted without direct written permission from the author or the publisher. Under no circumstances will any blame or legal responsibility be held against the publisher, or author, for any damages, reparation, or monetary loss due to the information contained within this book, either directly or indirectly.

Legal Notice:

This book is copyright protected. It is only for personal use. You cannot amend, distribute, sell, use, quote or paraphrase any part, or the content within this book, without the consent of the author or publisher.

Disclaimer Notice:

Please note the information contained within this document is for educational and entertainment purposes only. All effort has been executed to present accurate, up to date, reliable, complete information. No warranties of any kind are declared or implied. Readers acknowledge that the author is not engaged in the rendering of legal, financial, medical or professional advice. The content within this book has been derived from various sources. Please consult a licensed professional before attempting any techniques outlined in this book. By reading this document, the reader agrees that under no circumstances is the author responsible for any losses, direct or indirect, that are incurred as a result of the use of the information contained within this document, including, but not limited to, errors, omissions, or inaccuracies.

Erotic Short Sex Stories

Table of Contents

Curvy Body Is Love..7

Idiot To A Virgin..27

A Deathly Quiet Room 45

Own Path To Adventure 61

A Nerd Was Awesome 82

A special Weekend...98

A Satisfied Smile...118

Relationship Is Much Harder 136

Erotic Short Sex Stories

Curvy Body Is Love

I'm not what you'd call a fantastic woman. I quickly found that I enjoyed sex after creating the type of curvy body which made guys want to have sex with me. I am by no means a perfect ten. I'm cuter than sexy, but I have an above-average bra size, thick lips that are always wrapped around a tough cock and I have a willingness to spread my thighs.

Some folks would call me simple. Others could call me a slut. I'm not denying being either. Most of the things they say about me are accurate. Yes I've sucked my fair share of cocks, been fucked by my fair share of guys and even let some of them splatter their hot cum all over my skin.

However, I'd been on a one on one basis every time. Some of these may have been one night stands, a number of them may have had girlfriends, but the number of individuals involved consistently remained at two. Yet I will admit—or nearly admit as long as I've had sex—I've played around with the dream of having sex with more than one man at the same time.

It'd never be just a dream. I mean what type of woman would do this type of thing? What type of slut would allow guys to fuck her like this? Just considering it flipped my lacy thong into a wet mess.

I believe my first experience with the notion of a gangbang arrived in the kind of reading my dad's dirty magazines. The very first time I responded with disgust, however, the second time I found myself at home and took the stash out, then began flipping through them. I wished to be the woman from the centerfold. I wished to be like the girls I discovered from the tales in the trunk. Girls that had sexual sex, much more enjoyable than my awkward and unsatisfying sex life at the moment. The story that stood out for me was based around a girl who went camping with her husband. They bunch made a couple of friends and one thing led to another with five guys fucking her, filling her with cum.

The following experience came in the shape of a porn movie among my immature man friends who'd put on during a party. In the lady's bleached blonde hair to her giant fake tits, everything about it dropped into the class of fake. Certainly not a turn on like the aforementioned narrative, but seeing her take on four giant cocks somehow made the dream a little more genuine.

The most recent experience with the concept of a gangbang came not too long after my own graduation. Really right after. That night everybody gathered for celebrations, a crazy night for certain but I don't think anybody needed a wilder night compared to my friend Becky. At one of those parties she ended up sucking off half a dozen men and fucking four of them. As soon as I heard the story I responded with disgust, but deep down inside me, I wished that it'd been me.

But I did not want the entire town knowing I'd allowed a bunch of guys to bang me. Becoming simple or a slut is something you'd be able to write off as being youthful. Obtaining a gangbang follows you about. You'll visit the grocery store and a person will recognize you as that chick that let four guys fuck you.

However, I couldn't stop thinking about the dream. It was the dream I believed about late at night once I found myself alone in my area without a man to phone over. An enjoyable dream, but nothing I would ever make become a reality. Or so I thought.

"I thought it would only be a girls' weekend," I started when Ashley put down her mobile phone. Following a messy breakup, I wasn't in the mood to take care of any member of the male species.

"I understand, but I didn't believe Tyler would be in the city."

She looked at me, then took a sip of her vodka and cranberry. We'd been home sitting at her aunt's beach condo and put a significant dent in her liquor. I wasn't certain how she intended to conceal that, but she didn't appear to be overly worried.

"What do you really need me to perform? Tell him he can't come over? That will go down nicely. I'm sorry."

"I'm so sorry, I'm in this crabby mood," I muttered.

"They will only be here for a little while, then they're heading out to town."

"Who is they?"

While I debated the severe ideas about not dating, Tyler did possess some appealing buddies; older, more mature, sexy college men. Perhaps I could hold off the relationship vow of silence for now.

"I'm not sure. He said 'we' while we were on the telephone. He didn't mention who was included."

I expected it comprised of James. James, while he wasn't the school quarterback, seemed like he could've been using a well-built figure and was a man next door with great looks.

"Just how long are they likely to be here?" I asked.

"He didn't say."

"Damn you," I stated with a grin as the funk encompassing me began to lighten up.

I hurried to my bedroom and dug through my purse. We spent all afternoon on the shore, and after a hot shower, I wore a set of old football shorts and a raggedy tank top. Not precisely the type of clothing I'd considered the dress to impress collection. I didn't pack much, but I made the mistake of packaging more bikinis than real clothes. I discovered a more straightforward tank top, a set of jean shorts and washed underwear, just in case.

I quickly brushed my hair, put on some makeup and managed to put on the shorts as the doorbell rang.

Since Ashley opened the door, I peeked through my bedroom door. Tyler came in with a case of beer and a kiss for Ashley. James followed closely and I stepped into the hallway with a grin. He seemed just like what I'd have over my commanding, nevertheless cheating ex-boyfriend. Then two guys came in who were equally new to me. I started wondering just who my doctor prescribed for me.

Tyler introduced them to Devon and Rick. Devon looked like the poor boy my mother would despise, finished with tattoos all over him and rugged, jet black hair. Rick appeared more like a man I could really see myself in a relationship. I narrowed down my choices to James and Devon.

The initial plan had them only sticking around to get some drinks before going Downtown to a few pubs.

Initially, I didn't really enjoy that program, however, after a couple of drinks, I changed my mind. They immediately reminded me why I'd been pissed off at the male members of the species. They hit on me and stared at my tits to the stage it became uneasy. I'll admit in the beginning I enjoyed the focus. It felt great to be reminded there were other guys on the market, but it quickly became more than that. I wished to cope with this particular weekend. I'd been glad Ashley was outside on the balcony and they would be departing shortly.

"I will be right back. Do you need anything?" Ashley asked as she slid open the sliding glass door.

"Another drink?" I'd been pacing myself, but they left me wanting to consume more.

"You have it?"

I believed she'd be back following a couple of minutes. How long could a stop in the restroom along with a boil at the kitchen take? I didn't have a third eye, but it looked like it took far longer than it should've taken. After Devon undressed me with his eyes for the third time in a moment, I decided to take things into my own hands for my beverage.

Since I opened the sliding glass door, I recognized Tyler had gone missing from the balcony. I feared the worst and my fears were confirmed when I saw that Ashley's white bedroom door was shut.

I didn't know what to do besides getting another beverage. I just didn't need to return on the porch, but the condominium didn't leave any other place else to conceal myself. Before I could make a decision the three of them joined me in the kitchen.

They included me in the conversation about shores, but I hardly took part in the other than nodding my head. My mind told me they were unattractive, but I understood they needed me. I'd be lying if I said I didn't need every one of them.

I sensed my body temperature increasing and I couldn't be certain if it was due to those three sexy men facing me, the air conditioning, or that I couldn't maintain myself at all. I envisioned being in bed with James. Sex with him could be a satisfying exercise. Devon would love to do something kinky, pushing me beyond what I felt comfortable doing. Rick would go out of the way to be certain he fulfilled me until he arrived.

All three of these had solid points, but I couldn't just grab them by the arms and drag them to the bedroom. Okay, maybe I really could, but it would be quite embarrassing for the other two.

My second thought wished I could blame the alcohol, nevertheless, I hardly needed a hot buzz. I pictured myself in bed with all three of them spread out around me, all of them nude, rock hard and ready for me. The idea left my cotton panties moist.

As they talked about fishing I completely stopped listening. What could it actually be like to own all three of these guys? Would I like it if they used me? Thinking these thoughts made me squirm from the counter. I took a long sip of my brightly colored, blended beverage and expected none of them had found my delight.

How can I do it? Can I just tell them I was miserable and wanted to get fucked?

The excitement in my body grew and my heart began to pound.

How would they respond? Imagine if I simply invited them to accompany me to the bedroom? Or could I simply drop to my knees on the kitchen tile?

I probably could've dropped to my knees since Ashley totally abandoned me. The next time two people were lonely, I intended to mention a couple of things to her. However, I didn't know how long they'd be. They'd not seen each other for a couple of weeks and probably needed to compensate for lost time. Part of the reason why I didn't want to encounter Tyler was due to their relationship. They'd been a happy couple that couldn't get enough of each other. Ashley and I were only eighteen, but I could see both of them getting married.

I didn't have a problem finding men. So far, however, after a couple of things always became dull to find or I found other reasons to finish the relationship. I wasn't prepared to repay, but I knew there was more than only one night stands and flings. Yet every one of them stood around me. I didn't need a relationship. I wanted to get fucked.

What would Ashley say if she came out and watched me hanging over the sofa and they were lining up to fuck me? What would she say following morning when she came outside and found us lost with my bedroom door shut?

She understood about my flings and about my one night stands. But she didn't understand about this dream.

I could feel the blood flood through my veins. My panties clung into my wetness. It might either remain as a dream or it may turn into a reality.

I took a long sip of my drink, nevertheless barely buzzed. I took a deep breath. I leaned back from the counter and pushed my chest out. "Guys, I'm really fucking horny."

The conversation stopped mid-sentence. All three of them turned to look at me and their mouths dropped.

"What do you really wish to do about it?" Devon said, immediately recovering from the surprise, coming back to his old self.

"I wish to get fucked." I couldn't think that the words had come from out of my mouth.

"I would be pleased to assist you with that." He stepped towards me.

I put my hands up to stop him. "From all three of you."

I have said some slutty things, but nothing could ever top that.

The three of them looked at each other. It didn't feel real. I walked between Devon and James towards my bedroom. My bare feet touched the tile, then the carpet since I moved in my room, but it felt like walking on air.

They followed me into my room with James being the last to enter. I looked at him and he closed the door. For some reason the ornaments on the walls were all shore and nautical items such as seashells along with a compass which seemed like it would burst into a classic vessel. I didn't think of anything for a few minutes. Time stood still and they looked like predators about to strike their prey. I felt like a slice of meat and I grinned.

They stepped forward and I stepped back, then dropped onto the mattress. This was the mattress where it would occur where my dream would become a reality.

It began with palms. I felt a set of hands-on the buttons of my shorts. I felt another set of hands disturb my tank shirt. I looked up and watched Devon between my thighs along with Rick's hands pulling up my tank shirt to reveal my orange bra.

I wished I'd thought to wear a matching bra and underwear, but I didn't believe that mattered to them. Everyone looked at me, their eyes full of lust. A massive bulge formed within Devon's jeans.

My shorts came off and my purple underwear followed. A brand new set of palms joined in. I watched James set his hands between my thighs and felt his hands brush across my lips. I let out a soft moan. He told me to be silent, that I didn't want Ashley to listen, but I knew one way or the other she'd learn about this. He slipped a finger into me and rubbed his thumb across my sensitive clit. My tender moan became loud. I held my tongue as a last-ditch attempt.

A couple of moments after my tits were outside the cups of my bra. They didn't even bother to remove my tank top or bra all the way down. Rick's mouth found my nipple and I let out a shout as he bit it. His palms weren't as gentle as his mouth. I typically hated, really despised when guys went for my tits, but this time it turned me on.

When Rick took my nipple out of his mouth, he continued sucking on it. I watched Devon again as he stood between my thighs with his trousers and boxers down at his knees, directing his rock hard cock towards me moist center.

I understood then that I hadn't mentioned condoms. Following the breakup, I didn't believe I'd be needing them for some time, so I didn't keep any stashed away somewhere. I was on the pill instead, and unprotected sex wasn't brand new to me, but these three men were people I hardly knew. I understand that should've freaked me out, but it only turned me on more. I wanted to feel them inside me, leaving nothing to divide us. I wanted them all to cum inside me.

I stared at my legs and observed as Devon stepped ahead. Time seemed to slow down as I felt his penis touch my moist lips. It felt as though I could feel every cell of him merge with my own. It made my entire body twist with delight. He pushed into me and time returned to normal.

My wetness enabled him to easily push into me. He filled me, giving my whole body a sense of passion as I'd never felt before. There was no turning back now.

He grabbed my buttocks. I wrapped my palms around him for comfort as he started to thrust into me. I bit my lip, but I couldn't curb my moans.

He fucked me for a moment or two, but until he came anywhere near to a climax, he resigned. Before I knew what was happening, I felt the following cock enter me. I looked up and saw James. My dream would come true. With him and two other men, this is something I wouldn't forget. I'll admit there could've been a single night where I had sex with my boyfriend at that time and churn out after that night to meet up with a different man. I'd thought of this as among the sluttiest of things I'd done, but it didn't even compare.

His thrusts got harder as everyone started to breathe harder. It was better than the exercise I'd imagined. He filled me with joy.

Right as I began to completely love it, he resigned. I found Rick coming up next. All three of these guys must've been talking, but I didn't recall any noise other than the hum of the air conditioner, the squeaking of the metallic framework and my extremities.

Devon and James left me to whine about the size department, however, Rick stood vertical and markedly bigger. He pushed into me and I could feel myself stretching to adopt him. I raised my grasp on the duvet as he began to thrust into me.

It wasn't a dream anymore. It was nowhere close to that now, but three guys were fucking me precisely at the same time. I was gangbanging. I wasn't the run of the mill slut anymore.

I wanted more. When James pulled out, I flipped over and stayed on my hands and knees. I didn't have to mention anything else. Someone took me from behind. I didn't know who it was initially until I looked back and watched Devon thrust. Rick came to my entrance. He knelt on his knees and put his penis near my mouth.

I licked his swollen head, tasting a hint of his salty precum. I opened my mouth and took him between my lips. I took him deep into my mouth while another guy fucked me. It didn't seem real. I sensed another set of hands-on my waist. Rick started fucking my mouth., using my mouth as my pussy. They used me for their pleasure and I adored it.

At some stage the enjoyment of a penis inside me, the sensation of a cock sliding between my lips and a set of hands me, made me drop. The delight overwhelmed my body. I closed my eyes and the orgasm erupted inside me used a huge force I'd never felt before. I didn't understand who I had in my mouth. I didn't know who'd been fucking me. The sensation sent me into a completely different world of enjoyment.

My orgasm was linked with another. I felt two controlled thrusts and in the last minute he pulled from me. I heard a grunt and understood that it'd been James behind me. Moments later I felt cum splatter onto my back. The hot, thick cum struck me so hard it nearly made me jump. He covered my butt with his cum.

Devon grabbed my head and pushed his cock down my throat. I didn't gag after as his succulent cum flooded my mouth. After he pulled back, I swallowed everything whole.

I wasn't done yet. I desired Rick. I desired his massive cock to satisfy me with his cum. I flipped myself over while the other two started putting their clothes back on. Rick nevertheless was nude from the waist down, his big cock still prepared for me.

He pushed me to the middle of the mattress and joined me. He climbed on top and took me. He didn't start off slow this time. He slammed his cock into me with everything he had. I moaned and cried out as his joy stuffed me, fucking me as though I was his slut.

I ended up together with him and rode him since it felt like the final cock I would get. I didn't just sit there. My entire body bounced up and down on his penis. I did what I could, shifting my entire body before he eventually gave me exactly what I desired.

As a powerful orgasm stuffed me, as my body began to stiffen while I arched my back, he pushed and unleashed a torrent of cum. My body shook into a blissful orgasm.

He rolled me off him after he was spent. I wasn't his girlfriend. I'd been some slut he and his friends had only fucked. They left me, my entire body sore and tired, drenched with sweat and cum still clinging to me. I could feel his cock throbbing inside me once I heard the front door open, then shut. I could taste the cum in my mouth. They fucked me, they used me. And I loved it. I felt dirty, I felt like a slut, I felt alive.

A couple of minutes after I heard a soft knock on my door. "Kayla?" Ashley asked.

"Yeah?" I said, getting up and donning a bathrobe.

"Could I come in?"

"Come."

"Are you OK?" Her face had a look of concern.

"Yeah." I couldn't hide my smile. I felt like I was shining.

"What happened?"

"Should I tell you?"

"And you're fine with it?"

"Yeah."

"You're such a slut."

We both giggled.

"I can't disagree with this."

"I never believed you'd do something like this. How can it be?"

"Words can't explain it."

I handed her the box score outline. Her mouth fell as I told how one man took me from behind while the other stuffed my mouth. Nevertheless, I think I saw a portion of her wanting to do it.

Idiot To A Virgin

Rose didn't want to be here.

She would rather be home sleeping her whole day away. But that would mean placing herself in direct opposition with her mother, the First Lady of a church, and her father, a very devout Christian who has been building up his reputation as a pastor for the past eight years. It wasn't like she'd asked to be born into a family so religious, but here she was, an eighteen-year-old blonde who was yet to have any of the liberties that comes with adulthood.

If she had her way, she wouldn't be here, clad in an outrageously modest skirt and a long-sleeved top, without the slightest touch of makeup on her face. She hated to go about flaunting her freckles. She wouldn't be so bothered if there were only a few of them sprayed across her nose. But no, she had much more than she considered normal. However, a touch of make-up was unacceptable because she needed to be 'Christ-like' when she went out to declare the gospel with her parents.

Being a pastor's daughter didn't have to be so hard, or did it? She had a feeling that all of this would be different and a whole lot easier to live with if they resided in one of those big cities. But here they were, in a small town filled with judgmental self-loathing people who only felt good about themselves when they made someone else feel like shit. Her skirt was a few inches past her knees. If it was a little shorter, everyone would speak ill of the pastor's daughter and her overly dramatic mom would cry, speaking of how her 'impropriety' had brought shame to their blameless family and a reproach to the Lord.

Rose knew all of that. She'd been there before, and sadly, it wasn't a situation she wanted to face ever again.

Eager to escape the scorching sun, she counted down to when she would return home. She hated the burning sensation on her feet as the sun's heat slipped through the spaces in her sandals, roasting her legs like barbecue.

Too lost in her thoughts to pay attention to the ground she walked on, she didn't realize there was a fist-sized stone in her path until she kicked it with her left foot. She jumped and yelped, but held back from cursing. In her moment of disorientation, her Bible slithered away from her grasp and landed on the hard, dusty ground.

"Oh, great!" She rolled her eyes as she bent over to pick up the book.

"You alright, Rose?" the girl beside her asked.

Rose turned sideways with a stiff smile. "Of course. Why wouldn't I be?"

"Well, I'd say you didn't wanna be here."

Rose had begun walking again, but Naomi's words had her stopping dead in her tracks.

"I'm sorry if my words were offensive," Naomi said.

"No," Rose said. "That's not it."

She thought for a moment, her eyes never leaving Naomi's. Not even for a moment had she thought that her real emotions could peek through her false front. She could have sworn the boredom she felt was anything but obvious. She'd always thought that a polite smile and a feigned display of zeal was all she needed to fool her family, the church, and even herself into thinking she was a saint. Now though, with Naomi's comment about her not wanting to be here, she wondered how much of her emotions were out in the open. And more importantly, who else could see these things besides Naomi.

A voice in her head told her there was no cause for alarm. Naomi after all was the person she was closest to. The girl was not only a member of the church but was also her cousin. So, Rose would be a damned good actress to pretend for so long around a girl who claimed to have Sherlock Holmes" kind of mastery over the science of deduction.

"That obvious?" Rose asked after staying silent for what could have been forever.

"Probably not." Naomi shrugged. "I guess it's because we have a lot more in common than you think."

"Are you saying…"Rose trailed off with a smile.

"Yes, May. I, just like you, do not have a heart for these things. Now that we are done with high school, hopefully, our overly religious parents will let us study in those big cities and we'll get to be who we truly are."

Naomi chucked. Rose did too.

"Probably even consider a change of name," Naomi added with a shrug.

"Probably?" Rose laughed harder, and then she frowned. "No, definitely. I do not like the name Rose."

She had never liked the name Rose, even when she was way younger. When Naomi had chosen to call her May instead, the girl had instantly become her favorite person. She should have known they had a lot more in common.

"Of all names though, they had to call you Rose." Naomi clicked her tongue, distaste evident in her eyes as she made a face.

"What am I? Some girl who got pregnant before getting to taste how damned good a cock is?"

"Hush!" Naomi turned around. "We are toast if they hear us talking about things like these."

"Yeah, right."

"You expecting anyone?" Trey asked, glancing sideways at his brother Devin.

Devin shook his head, but didn't look away from the television screen in front of him.

The brothers were in the final minutes of a football match and in Trey's moment of distraction, he knew his brother would gain the upper hand. He glanced at the door. He didn't have a lot of friends, so no one ever came to visit him. He wasn't complaining or anything though. He had his PlayStation 4 to keep him company, and then there was Devin his brother.

Just like him, Devin didn't have a lot of friends, unless you counted the girls who came visiting because they couldn't get enough of his cock. He had seen his brother's cock more times than he could remember, so he knew just why the girls couldn't stop coming. Truth be told, they would always beat a path to their door. If there was anything Devin invested in, it was his body. While he worked hard to build up the rest of his body, he never left out his cock. Trey had walked in on him using penis pumps and cock enlargement creams a couple of times, so he could say that Devin's cock was way bigger than it used to be. The extra length and girth

Devin's cock had earned could make Trey want to enhance his own cock as well, but at eight inches long, he didn't think there was a need for any of that.

"Think they're gone now?" Trey asked.

Devin shrugged, too engrossed in the match to say another word.

Trey set down his console and proceeded to open the door. His face paled at the sight of two women in front of him. Although he had never seen them before, he knew at once who they were. They were dressed in outrageously modest outfits, their hair stuck beneath tight scarves, but the locks of hair peeking through told him they were blonde-haired. As though their outward display of propriety wasn't enough to announce that they were 'Followers of Christ, they had their Bibles to make it all clear. And he was not one to listen to the doctrines of these people.

"Good afternoon," the first of them said.

"Not interested!" Trey moved to shut the door, but the second blonde made a frantic effort to stop him.

"You won't even see what we have to offer?" she asked.

"I already told you…" he started, and then he smiled. "Oh my, pardon my rudeness."

Was he thinking of sending them away? Beneath their extreme modesty, he saw the beauty in their eyes. The girls were young, probably younger than his twenty years of age. He glanced behind them and there was no other preacher insight. Their church was stupid to leave two young girls unguarded. It was a sight Trey didn't see too often, and he had no idea when next he would get another chance like this.

"Oh, it's okay," the first girl said. "I am Naomi and my sister—"

"May," the second said, flashing him an almost enchanting smile.

"Wanna come in?" he asked. "There is so much I wanna know."

He stepped aside and opened the door wider, letting the unsuspecting girls into his house. He grinned as Devin glanced at him with a face wrinkled with confusion. And when he winked at Devin, Devin responded with a knowing smile. They had always joked about teaching preachers a lesson, and the girls looked good enough to fuck.

Trey closed the door behind him. "By the way, I'm Trey, and this is my brother, Devin."

Devin winked at them. The girls smiled. Or were they blushing? Trey could have sworn their cheeks reddened when Devin winked at them. He had a feeling that beneath the layers of clothing was a sultriness he would love to explore.

"Please sit." He gestured at a couch.

"Thank you," the girls chorused.

They sat beside each other, and the second girl engaged him in a conversation he didn't want to be a part of. Her name was May, he remembered. He sat on the armrest of Devin's couch, and while he pretended to listen to May, Devin couldn't be bothered about any of that. He didn't take a break from his game. Well, at least he turned down the volume of the TV.

Trey knew he had to act. He didn't think the girls were allowed to spend so much time away from the other church members. He would hate the moment to pass without him getting to do what he had always dreamed of. So when the girls started to read scripture, he knew there was no better time to act.

"I should come close so I can read along," he said.

He rose from beside Devin and proceeded to sit beside May. He liked that one. She was blonde, blue-eyed and very beautiful. Even her unfashionable outfit couldn't make her any less beautiful.

"Come over here you idiot," Trey said to Devin.

Devin feigned reluctance, and then he sat beside Naomi. All four of them were slender, so they could fit into the couch. It was a tight space though. Just perfect.

"Now, Trey, I was saying..." May resumed where she left off, but Trey didn't give her a chance.

He plucked the Bible out of her hands and placed it on the stool on his side of the chair. Before May could say a word, he covered her lips with his.

She withdrew from him. "What are you doing?"

He slipped his left hand between her legs, groping her pussy through her skirt.

"Please..." she moaned.

Was she begging for him to stop or for him to fuck her already? Trey decided that she was begging him to continue. There was an undiluted lust in her eyes. From the corner of his eye, he could see Devin kissing Naomi just as hard. The girl, just like May, was also putting up feigned resistance. But she should know she didn't stand a chance against a man as robust as Devin.

Trey covered May's body with his and yanked down her skirt.

"Please, wait—" May cried, still feigning resistance.

She made an attempt to vacate the chair, but he slammed her back down and ripped off her panties. He hadn't expected the fabric to rip so easily, but it did anyway, bringing her pussy into full view. She tried to clamp her legs shut but he peeled them apart and buried his head between them. His tongue slipped right in, past her pussy lips.

"Oh, yes...s" She shamelessly moaned.

The girl was wet between her legs, her pussy lips swollen with what could have been arousal. He reached deeper with his tongue, and then he started to flick it around, mixing his spit with her pussy juice.

"Please!" she cried. "Show me the true meaning of pleasure. It doesn't matter that I'm the Pastor's daughter."

Trey paused. "Really?"

May nodded.

"I'll fuck you until you ask for more!" He glued his right index finger and his pointer together and shoved them inside her.

She cried and jumped from sheer pleasure, but he pinned her down, shoving his fingers deeper until they could go no further.

"I am a virgin, you idiot!" she snapped. "I wouldn't want to be limping when I join others!"

"Well, there's a way around that!" Trey said.

With his fingers still inside her, he yanked down his pants, bringing his huge cock out of hiding. He grabbed her left leg and hung it over the armrest of the chair so her ass was in full sight. Her tight ass didn't have the luxurious wetness of her pussy, but he could fix that with his spit.

"Are you a virgin as well?" he heard Devin ask.

"I'm not a pastor's daughter," Naomi replied with a chuckle.

Trey glanced at her and found her parting her legs to let Devin in. She moaned as Devin slipped inside her. His cock throbbing with anticipation, Trey returned his attention to May and was stunned find her rubbing her own pussy and moaning quite loudly.

"Virgin, huh?" He raised a brow.

"I'm trying to open up my ass to let your cock you idiot!" she hissed.

For a girl so pretty, she had a flaring temper, and for a preacher's daughter, she was one hell of a bitch. Trey wasn't complaining though. He wanted to fuck her hard enough to leave her sore for talking at him in that manner. Her temper would make him do just that, without an ounce of regret for being so hard on her.

No girl had ever called him an idiot. Much less a stranger.

Fueled by a need to make her pay for bruising his ego, he decided against spitting on his cock to ease the friction when he slipped into her ass. He planted his cock at her entrance, pinning her down as he thrust right in.

There was no building up or going easy.

He thrust hard enough to tear her anal muscles as if they were made of fabric as light as her panties. Lucky her, they weren't.

May's soft moans filled his ears as he shoved his cock inside her. She squirmed, whimpering as she tried to fill her asshole with his big cock but then, Trey wanted to be the one controlling the pace, and not her. She made another loud seductive moan and Trey almost lost himself in pleasure. He grabbed her arms, pinned them to the chair and tried to shove his full length inside her. Her ass clenched hard around him and her eyes hardened, flashing with emotion he recognized as ecstasy. He knew that she was enjoying every bit of his ministrations. Her shivering body and her moans had betrayed her.

"Jesus, Trey!" she gasped. "Is this all you fucking got?"

Trey looked up into her eyes, and then he smirked. He knew her type. He knew that although she was already in the cocoon of sexual bliss, she wanted him to feel like a lesser man.

"No," he said. "But thanks for asking."

He heaved her off the couch and slammed her down on the floor. Without giving her a moment to adjust to her new posture, he flipped her over so she lay flat on her chest. He grabbed her hips and yanked them toward his body. She responded with a whimper as he forced her on all fours. She didn't even try to move away. It was as if she was faithfully waiting for his dick to claim her asshole. Without lingering any longer, he thrust into her ass and wrapped her hair around his fingers. He started to thrust in and out, tugging at her hair with each thrust.

May was moaning now, her ass clenching and unclenching. She breathed hard and fast, as though she'd been in a marathon.

Trey chuckled. "Funny how I am yet to fully enter you and you're already moaning."

He spanked her ass.

"Is it in yet?" she asked.

"What the fuck?"

"Sorry, I can't help it. You're just so tiny that I don't know if you're fully inside—"

She was trying to make him fuck her harder with her words and he knew it. The bitch sure loves a good cock.

Trey slammed hard, shoving his full length inside her with one fluid move. May swallowed the rest of her words. All Trey could hear was a soft cry of pleasure, and then there was another, a much louder cry as he started to pound.

"Oh Trey," May cried. "Please fuck me harder. Don't you—"

A knock at the door cut her off.

"Shit!" she whispered. "My father?"

"Who is it?" Devin asked voice raised.

Trey glanced back and found him balls-deep in Naomi's tight pussy, slowly thrusting.

"Just the local pastor," a man said from behind the door. "Have any preachers come this way?"

"You know," Trey whispered, tugging so hard at May's hair that her head dipped backward, toward him, "I could say yes and ask him to come in."

"Please don't." She shook her head.

"Give me a reason not to." He loosened his hold on her.

She crawled away, and then she turned around to lay on her back. She parted her legs, her hands reaching between them to part her pussy lips.

"Fuck my pussy," she said.

"Hello?" the pastor called again.

"No preachers!" Devin yelled back.

Trey crawled toward May and crept between her legs. He held her thighs apart, kissing her lips as he mounted her. She kissed him back, her lips soft and moist.

"Do you really want this?" he asked. "Do you want to lose it to me, May?"

Trey had no explanation for this, but for the first time since he got naked with May, this wasn't about teaching her a lesson. There was something different and he didn't know what it was.

"Do you?" he asked again.

She nodded.

Trey heaved his body off her and helped her to her feet. "Pick a date."

"Tonight. I'll be here."

"Promise?"

She nodded, an innocent smile creeping to her face. "Promise."

A Deathly Quiet Room

The phone rang incessantly. Wondering why Lana didn't answer it, I rolled over, searching blindly for the receiver.

"Hello," I mumbled.

"Wake up, Ryan. Wake up!" Her voice was strident.

"Who is it?"

"Mary Jane. Do you know where Lana is?"

I looked around.

Where the hell was Lana?

"Ryan!" Mary Jane shouted. "It's two thirty in the morning. Where is your wife?"

"I don't know."

"I do. She's at Bart's house pulling a train. Do you know what that means? She's gangbanging all your so-called friends. You're a laughing stock. A cuckold too stupid to know his wife is cuckolding him. Wake up, Ryan!"

"I am awake."

"No, you're not. Everyone knows about her but you, and everyone who knows her does her. Do you like being married to the biggest slut in town?" she said, her voice low and cold.

"No."

"That's what she is. She did Bart the night before your wedding. She did some guy she met on the beach while you were on your honeymoon and bragged about it when she got back. Now she's doing all of them. How does that make you feel?"

"Shitty," I said. "Really low and shitty."

"Maybe there's hope for you yet," she replied. "Good night, Ryan. I'll pray for you," she said before hanging up.

In less than a minute, I was dressed and running for the car. In less than ten minutes, I tried Bart's front door, but it was unlocked. I quietly let myself in and tiptoed to the living room. A bunch of them were sitting around naked, drinking beer and shooting the shit.

There was Bart in his easy chair—one of my two best friends. A groomsman at our wedding. I knew Bart would fuck anything, but I thought he'd leave my wife alone out of friendship if nothing else. His wife, Betty, was a sweet and giving woman. I liked her, but she was a certified slut. Hell, I slept with her before she dated Bart and she had offered herself to me regularly since then. I knew they were wife swappers because both of them had approached me about Lana and me joining their club.

There were my other friends—Andy, Bill, Jack, Little Jeff and Pctc.

Betty, wearing a sweatshirt that covered everything to her crotch, came in from the kitchen with two beers in each hand. She saw me and froze. "Hello, Ryan," she said.

The room got deathly quiet. I looked at each of them, but they wouldn't look at me.

"Where's Lana?" I asked.

"In the bedroom with Big Jeff and Mike," Betty replied.

Just then Mike came through the door from the hall. "Next," he announced with a big shit-eating grin. He saw me and sagged back against the wall with his mouth hanging open. Mike—my other best friend and brother-in-law. I knew Amy, my sister, didn't know about her husband fucking the town slut. Amy would cut off Mike's nuts if she knew.

"Don't blame us. We're not the only ones she's fucking," Bill said.

"Yeah, Ryan. If she's giving it away, why shouldn't your friends get some? She's the best I've ever had," Bart added. Betty looked pissed off, but the guys mumbled in agreement.

Bart was right. Lana was built like a brick shithouse and had a wild, demanding sensuality when she wanted sex, which was a lot of the time. She'd get a look in her eye—a supernatural look like in a cartoon. No man could resist that look. She loved to fuck more than any woman—hell, more than any man—I ever met. And good? Bart was right again. Lana was the best.

"What's been happening?" I asked.

"She's been here since one, taking all of us any way we want it," Mike answered.

"Who came in her mouth?" I asked.

Four hands went up, two of them from Andy. "The other hands for Big Jeff," he said sheepishly.

"In the ass?"

"She told us she'd tell our wives if we did her like that," Bill replied.

"Shit. She told us she'd cut us off and that's even worse," Pete snickered.

No anal sex. Period. That was Lana's rule. She'd do anything but that, and if I ever had her ass, she'd never speak to me again.

I saw Bart give Betty a signal. She handed out the beers except for one and brought it to me. I took a swig as

Betty's hand slipped under my tee shirt and slid across the top of my jeans. "Let's go somewhere and talk, Ryan," she said seductively.

"No thanks, Betty. I want to join in my wife's gangbang."

"Oh, that's great," someone said and they all begin to talk, like someone had turned on the electricity and a display started. The pressure was off them. I wasn't an angry husband. I was one of the guys participating in fucking the slut.

"I'm going to fuck her ass and you guys are going to help me," I said.

The electricity disconnected. All was quiet again.

"This is what's going to happen. I want her on the bed doggy-style. Mike, you'll hold her head. Pete and Little Jeff will hold her arms. Andy and Bart will hold her legs. I'll plow her from behind. You will hold her like I want her. Understand?"

"Not me," Bart said. "She's too good to give up." Bart didn't know it, but he just bought more trouble than he could handle.

"I'll take the other leg, Ryan. It's the least I can do for you," Jack said.

"That's right, guys. We owe it to Ryan. He's our buddy and he's always been there for us," Mike said. "Let's do it."

Lana was facing the far wall when we entered the bedroom. She was on her hands and knees on the bed with Jeff fucking her doggy-style, driving into her sloppy cunt with all he had. I heard her laugh—a demonic, guttural laugh—like she does when she orgasms. I wondered how many times she had.

Jeff drove hard into her. She pushed back against him and wiggled her hips. "That's it, Baby. Fill me up," she said.

That's what she always said when I came in her.

Mike crawled in front of her with his back against the headboard. Lana thought he wanted his cock sucked and her head dropped into his lap. The others took their places before she realized what was happening.

I pushed Jeff aside and took his place between her legs. His cum drooled out of her, or maybe it was Mike's cum, or whoever's it was. There was a pile of the wet sticky stuff on the sheet under her red and well-used pussy.

"I need a cock in me," she said, raising her head up to look Mike in the face. "Who's next?"

Mike tangled his hands in her hair above the ears on both sides of her face to get a good grip and pulled her head back until his face was near hers. "Ryan," he said.

The world stood still. No one made a sound.

"Ryan? My husband?"

I drove my cock into her loose and well lubed pussy. When I pulled out, there was as much cum on my cock as there was when we fucked at home.

"Yes, Lana. It's me," I said. "Hold still, baby. You're going to love this."

I drove all the way into her ass with one long, hard stroke, burying my cock in her bowels to the hilt. She screamed and started struggling. Lana's strong for her size and her adrenalin pumped, but she was tired from a hard night's fucking and six big guys held her in place.

All that twisting and fighting gave my crotch a good massage from her hips and her sphincter spasmed on my cock.

Any other time, all that stimulation would've made me go off like a Roman candle. This time, I wasn't even close. I wanted to do this my way.

She fought until she couldn't move. The guys were holding her up, not holding her still as she sucked in air by the bushels. I took a hip in each hand and slowly began to fuck her ass.

Something happened to her. It must've been the heat, exertion and continual sexual stimulation for a couple of hours. And the hard dick in her asshole, of course. I heard her demonic laugh, but it was different this time, like I'd heard only once before. It was staccato, like she was laughing with the hiccups. Lana was building to a mind-blowing climax.

"Listen," I barked. "Grab her tits, guys. Jack, do her clit. Andy, finger her. Mike, pull her hair. On the beat. Ready. Squeeze. Tug. Tug. Release. Rest. Squeeze. Tug. Tug. Release. Rest."

Betty started clapping the rhythm and chanting the words. The others not doing it chimed in. "Squeeze. Tug. Tug. Release. Rest."

Only Lana and I were off beat. She was twitching, rotating and growling. Her skin were on fire. She cursed and babbled incoherently. The guys holding her were working to keep her in place. The chanting got louder. "Squeeze. Tug. Tug. Release. Rest."

Me? I was driving up her dark hole and struggling to stay in her without cumming. The motions, heat and pressures were excruciating.

"Faster," I said. They picked up the tempo and so did Lana.

I heard her pre-climax laugh. She screeched and yanked herself free. She sat back hard, burying me in her. Her nails dug into my thighs. Her ass tightened on my cock.

It definitely was not fun. The pain was intense, like when you catch your dick in your zipper. I screamed.

Lana screamed, vomited on Mike, and passed out.

Lana stayed there. Betty said she'd take care of her. Pete and Little Jeff took me to the hospital. Dr. Booker was on duty. We all knew Helen, who was three years ahead of us in high school. I showed Helen the puncture wounds made by Lana's claws in my thighs and I showed her my dick.

"Ryan, your penis is horribly bruised. Doesn't it hurt?"

"It's killing me," I replied.

"I'll get some painkiller and an icebag. You can't have sex for a few weeks. Don't even masturbate. If it's not painfree in five days, you need to see me again. I'm going to cleanse and stitch your wounds." She glared at me. "Were these made by a woman?"

"Lana," I replied.

"I've seen wounds made when a woman clawed a man, but none like these. These are wider and deeper." She shook her head in disbelief and started the procedures.

The painkiller wiped me out. I barely remember the guys getting me home and in bed.

Someone shook me. I heard my name being called as I fought to clear the cobwebs from my mind.

"Wake up, Ryan," she said, shaking me again.

"Mom?" I mumbled. "What are you doing here?"

"You're not at home. You're in the hospital and you have been for two days."

Mom look terrified. So did Dad, Mike and Amy who were standing behind her. I turned my head to see Father Morris who looked more terrified and had a crucifix in his hand.

"In the name of the Father, the Son and the Holy Spirit. Amen," Father Morris said as he made the sign of the cross on my forehead.

"What's going on?" I asked.

"Lana's in the hospital, too. She almost died," Mom answered.

"Mike told us what happened at Betty's house. He told us everything," Amy said.

"Lana was possessed by the Devil," Father said. He sounded as scared as he looked. "The anal sex drove him from her body. At least that's what the exorcist thinks. We really don't know."

"They want you to be exorcised," Mom said.

"They want to exorcise all of us there that night," Mike interjected.

"Exorcise the Devil? You're kidding me?"

"The Devil isn't funny, Ryan," Father said piously.

Maybe not, but I snickered anyway. I went to Mass most Sundays and Confession three or four times a year, but I thought demonic possession was bullshit. I didn't say that to Father Morris though. He looked like he had enough problems. They stayed with me and talked for ten minutes or so before Dr. Booker came in.

"Time to leave. He needs his rest," she said. Mom kissed me and they all tottered off. Dr. Booker threw the covers back and checked my thighs. "You're healing more quickly than I expected."

"Good genes," I joked.

"I had the nurse remove the catheter. How's your penis feeling?" she asked. She bent over and took my cock in her hand. "Healing nicely, I see. I think this medicine is what it needs."

She sucked it in her mouth. That surprised me. I always thought of Helen as asexual, even when I was in high school and anything in skirts looked good. I didn't think of her that way as she bobbed on my cock giving me one hell of a good blowjob.

As her hand slowly worked my hard and needy shaft, she looked up at me. I knew that look. It was Lana's look—the one she had when she desperately needed sex.

Or was it the Devil's look?

"The priests are looking for me," Helen said, but it didn't sound like Helen. Her voice was low and guttural. "Don't tell them where I am and you'll have the best sex you ever had."

"I won't tell them," I said.

"That's my good boy," Helen said in that unworldly voice. She lowered her mouth to my cock. In seconds, I spurted my load and she swallowed it. "I'll be back," she said as she left me alone.

Why should I tell the priests? I knew what was happening now. If I managed it, the demon would jump from Helen to another woman when I was ready, so the best sex would be there for me. And I knew how to manage it. I could fuck the Devil away.

The nurse came in. She was a little plump, but that didn't matter. I stared at her. She looked terrified and helpless. A tear rolled down her cheek as she looked at her wedding rings. She shivered, locked the door, and removed her hose and panties.

"Take off everything," I said.

She nodded and undressed before climbing on the bed and impaling herself on my cock. I lay back with my arms behind my head and let her do the work. I was in no hurry. I liked watching her face and her bouncing tits. She humped until she was red-faced and near exhaustion. The room stunk of sex. Her pussy was getting dry and my crotch was soaked in her juices.

She didn't orgasm, but that wasn't important to either of us. Only one thing was important. My orgasm.

Clearly, she would fuck herself to death rather than stop before I climaxed.

When I let myself cum, I laughed. It surprised me, and I thought, "Jesus, was that my laugh?"

Own Path To Adventure

I was really looking forward to Beltane (May day), which for me is probably my biggest religious holiday of the year. Spending a few days celebrating openness, embracing passion and love, a break with my gods and community was just what I needed. April was tough.

Shortly before the festival, my girlfriend let me know that she wouldn't be able to come. In many ways, this was our event, the time when we get to be as together as we can be. However, a critical family emergency kept her away. Being all alone at a sex-related festival is very different from being there with a cherished lover, and I was having trouble adjusting. She was going to help me teach a class, and I wasn't sure who I could find that I'd trust enough to take on that role.

The weather looked discouraging.

I got on the plane and felt nervous, wondering how things would work out. Still, I was heading to the space where I first met Venus, where I first embraced spirituality and real openness.

What could go wrong?

I found out as the taxi turned off the highway about 45 minutes away from the airport. "Oh, fuck!" I said.

"What's wrong."

My stomach was knotted so tightly I couldn't get the words out for a few moments. On top of everything else, I just couldn't deal with this. "This isn't my bag."

For a few brief moments I considered abandoning my luggage and just go without for the festival, but replace everything later. The festival was clothing-optional; there isn't a lot I strictly had to have. Giving up that dream, I faced the long, expensive trek back to the airport and back to the camp ground. The driver was happy to tell me of the plans he'd already had to cancel to pick me up. He wasn't upset, we were both commiserating in our misery.

Eventually, I got to camp. I was a mess. I was stressed by life, and by the immediate logistics of getting there. I had no idea what I'd be doing or how I was going to teach my class. I didn't feel connected with myself or my spirituality.

A significant part of my spiritual path is working with an aspect of Venus. I experience her as a goddess of love and sexuality, particularly focused on transformation and growth through the more fiery aspects of love. I think there are times when she's sitting there in our hearts, or wherever we perceive her, smiling as she has an opportunity to nudge two people closer together, hoping they will be good for each other. Looking back on my arrival at camp, meeting Susan was one of those times. Susan was new to our cabin; she had been at the event before and was nervous about whether she would fit in and connect this time. I knew this because the person who brought her met me at check-in, anxious, hoping that I could help her feel welcome. I'd do my best.

She's there when I, exhausted and soul-weary, get to the cabin. I say hi and generally give people an update on my state. She suggests she might be able to help with my class.

We hang out. It could be warmer. Normally at such an event I'd be naked almost all of the time. Quickly, I find that I need at least a coat. I get to know her; she seems like someone I could work with. The group is trying to figure out whether to do anything or just head to bed.

Susan and I talked about needing to do a scene together if she's going to help. Part of what I'm looking for is a safety monitor for short scenes taking place in the class. I point out we could wander over to the play space and see how we work together. We're feeling each other out and discover we're both interested in doing that.

So, I find myself tied to a bench while someone I have known for less than four hours sorts through my toys. It's safe: there are monitors and the event organizer is screening on nearby equipment. The scene is physically intense, or at least, it feels that way. However, at another level, it's a very light scene: a combination of me giving instruction in how to explore and use my body with the use of surprise and a few other tricks. We are happy: she feels included and I've started to relax somewhat. We talk about the possibility of doing a scene with more complex intent later.

It's Friday. Susan helped with my class. It was a success. Really, that doesn't begin to describe it: the class became a cabin project and together we rocked the world inviting people to be open and challenge themselves. That, however, is another story.

She waunders over and asks, "Hey, want to go to the flogging ritual?" I think the class is called 'Driving Toward Ecstasy', but everyone calls it the flogging ritual. I've been interested in going for years, but never had a partner who I thought would be interested in topping or bottoming at that ritual.

"Sure, do you want to top or bottom?"

"Either."

Now I have to think. I feel like I've been submitting a lot so far, and feel like I ought to want to top. I don't though. I look within myself and find that my confidence is still fairly low from the month before. "If I had my preference I'd bottom. However, if there's something you need to do at the ritual, I can top. My confidence is still fairly low and it would be easier to bottom."

"Okay; you bottom. Will you supply toys?"

"Sure, I'll bring Mr. Thuddy and the small flogger."

Mr. Thuddy is the name for my wonderful, large, heavy flogger. Mr. Thuddy is not to be confused with Mr. Thud, that huge hunk of metal that the asshole in Connecticut keeps offering to hit people with at events, claiming he's 'got thud.'

New people think Mr. Thuddy is scary; you hand him to them, they feel the weight and think they aren't going to like that. Bashing people with the handle would in fact be rude. However, there are lots of wide straps, and the weight of the handle brings inertia into play: unless you're really strong, you're going to get a nice even stroke. So, you actually get a wonderful, relaxing thud with very little sting, except for on the wrap.

Because Susan does not identify as spiritual, I guess the experience will be more physically intense than spiritually intense. For me, thinking of flogging as leading to ecstasy is very easy. I find flogging, especially with a nice thuddy flogger, relaxing. It can almost be some form of deep massage. With very little ritual help to create space, and by staying in the moment and giving into the experience, I could easily see myself getting to an ecstatic high. I'm assuming it will be something like that.

I arrive. I'm standing in front of a St. Andrew's cross. It's an X-shape with rings to attach wrist and ankle restraints to. I have attached padded cuffs for my wrists but will not restrain my ankles.

I'm nervous. Susan is not there yet. I need to pee, and I go, but I'm worried about whether I'll need to pee again during the ritual. I'm worried about whether the wrist restraints are too high. It might seem silly to be worried about comfort when I'm about to get flogged. However, the point is to be open to the experience of the flogging, to experience that as fully as possible. Other discomforts can get in the way. Also, discomfort from restraints can be a sign of bad blood-flow or a pinched nerve, both of which are safety issues.

The time of the ritual approaches and Susan is not there. My nervousness grows. I'm not looking forward to sitting there and being unable to participate because I don't have a top.

I realize that I'm not doing well. The people at the festival have been wonderful; connections have deepened within our cabin especially. However, the festival itself has been challenging. A lot of it is the weather: it's been fucking cold with lots of rain. I don't mean fucking cold; cold that has to be defeated by warm bodies and lots of activity can be a lot of fun for Beltane. I mean it's so cold that the idea of getting undressed enough to fuck is entirely unappealing. I've been wearing most of what I brought (admittedly not much) the entire time, often wishing for more layers. Now, I'm standing only in a trench coat, hoping that when I take the coat off to be restrained to the cross, I won't be too cold to be naked. There are space heaters, but they don't seem to be doing much.

I have enough experience both with BDSM and with spirituality that I should be able to fight through the nervousness. I'm in a position of great strength. This is the room where I first made a vow to Venus. This is the room where I was first flogged for that matter. My people—my tribe—are here and all around me. I try to relax and open my senses. I smell the wood of the cross. In all probability I've tied people to this cross. For all I know it's the cross where … well, where some great growth happened. There's an even higher probability that I've been tied to this cross before. No matter what happens, I will be fine. I breathe, reaching to ground myself.

Susan sweeps in. She's the top; she can help. I'm not used to leaning on my top emotionally quite as much as I'm doing, but if she's up to helping, it will make things much easier. I've certainly been in the position of helping a bottom out before. She is up to it; she helps me check the restraints, I go to the bathroom one final time, and we're ready.

Everyone gathers in a circle. The ritual leader uses the same grounding exercise I incorporate into my rituals and as we breathe together, I find myself focusing, more centered, ready to open. That's the value of the aspects of ritual: through shared symbols we can train ourselves to quickly and easily enter into a shared experience and context. I've done this enough times that even when I'm near my worst, the words of a common spiritual path—combined with trust I have in the ritual leader and community—bring me to a place where I'm ready to be open, ready for an experience.

We discuss intent. The plan is for us to do chakra work—work focused on spiritual nodes of our body that tie us together and to the world around us. We will find things within ourselves, use the energy of the flogging to separate those parts we want to keep from those we need to discard. Then, in the climax of the ritual, we will release that which we no longer need so that it can be recycled back into the world.

Ah fuck, so much for my plan of a nice, simple physical experience with a ritual backing. What the ritual leader is describing is deep spiritual work. I briefly consider whether I'm really going to dive fully into that intent and try to do the deep work. I'm here, so I need to be here and this is the work I need to do. Later, of course, looking back on that reasoning, I'll see the holes in it. However, I'm in my spiritual home, in my community, in a place of safety. I'm in a place where I have chosen to be vulnerable, chosen to take risks. I have chosen to trust the people, the experiences and the gods of this place, this event. I have full confidence that no matter what happens, I will be safe. Even if I end up an emotional wreck at the end of the ritual, I can find people to help me. I'm here in part because I can be this open, because there is enough trust that when I need healing the most, I can trust enough to do it. That trust and confidence is something I've built up over the years.

Interestingly, if I had been doing better, I might have chosen to adapt my intent to something closer to what I had originally imagined, while still working within the overall intent. In part, because I recognize that I'm not at my best, I'm open to doing more intense work.

The ritual is set to popular music. The ritual leader has picked a playlist and will guide us through building the energy, using the music for rhythm, pacing and tone. As I would expect, the safety arrangements are good.

Susan and I return to our cross. I realize that I face the interesting challenge of working as a bottom to guide a top who is not spiritual through the process of creating a deeply spiritual experience for me. I never stop to think about whether I'll be able to do that, whether Susan will be able to do that, or whether she wants to. I trust her to look out for her own safety and needs: we had that conversation as part of the first scene we did. If she's uncomfortable she'll let me know. Instead, I focus on how I can help her accomplish that goal.

She's got everything under control. We touch and hug and the ritual begins.

She restrains my wrists and begins to connect with my body. There is touch, contact, warmth. Music plays; it is important to set a rhythm. However, it is important to my primal self; that part is greedy, my rational self doesn't even get a memory of the music. Still, it forms a baseline for what is to come.

We breathe through our feet. That is, we feel the ground under us, we reach out to the connections between us and the space, and as we breathe air, we also pull in and out the energy of those connections. We bring ourselves into alignment with the ground, with our sacred space through our feet. They support us; they bring us a source of power that we will use to do work.

As I begin to connect with my body, she caresses me with Mr. Thuddy: the wonder of leather against skin, soft supple straps gliding across my body, the rich smell of well-cured leather. The experience is sensual. I open to her as I open to my body. Our relationship is complex. I'm in her hands physically, I trust her to bring my body where I need to go; I have surrendered fully. Even though I have only known her for a couple of days, at this moment, I am hers. We know safe words and have discussed communication, but within my mind that's all hidden behind a break glass 'in case of emergency' mental box.

However, at another level I'm guiding her. Through signals, a few words, and allowing my body to be as expressive as I can, I'm going to lead her in creating an experience for me.

The music and ritual leader guide us to find and approach our chakras. I take a quick inventory. I expect to find problems with my heart, voice and possibly will.

While I'm taking inventory, let us take a step back and explore the last month. For the deep spiritual healing we're going for, details matter. I approach love as something that can be learned, practiced and taught. I'm working to build a spiritual group to do that, openly helping people explore love and sexuality, growing and learning as lovers. My best friend and I were on a trip exploring the possibility of someone else working with us. By the end of the trip, our friendship was destroyed, he had left the group, and I was doubting my ability to do the work. At the same time my girlfriend told me she would not be able to come to Beltane and warned me I'd be facing another challenge. A close friend planned to recommend that I was unfit for the path I had chosen; that I should not act as a priest.

That is the backdrop against which I took inventory of myself. I was shocked to find my root—my connection to self, to living in the present moment—was damaged. My second chakra—sexuality and openness to feelings and emotions—seemed entirely blocked. I couldn't detect anything. Somehow, I'd expected that since I'd felt these events as a challenge of love, of will, and of voice, that I would feel them there.

I am frightened. I don't even understand myself; how can I heal?

I call over my shoulder to Susan, "I'm going to be doing a lot of lower chakra work apparently. That's not what I expected."

I wonder if she knows what that means in some back corner of my mind. It doesn't matter though: part of the magic of the situation is that she will give me what I need. It's that way in part because I've decided it is. However, at a deeper level, her intent, her desire to give me the ritual I need, combined with my trust and openness to her, is driving the power of the ritual as much as any stroke of the flogger. The flogger is there to make that trust and vulnerability physically manifest.

She begins to hit gently. As I asked, she focuses on my lower body. She welcomes me with her lash.

The ritual leader invites us to begin exploring what we need to give up and what we need to keep. My feelings are first: I need them. They need to flow through me. Some I may discard, but I must feel them first. Mr. Thuddy's strands are still relatively gentle as they strike between my lower back and thighs, but they are sufficient. They cut through the emotional scabs separating me from my feelings.

I'm frightened. I can't do my spiritual work alone. Am I being asked to do that? How will I find someone else? What happens when I can no longer find people to connect with?

The connection my best friend and I had shared was the basis on which I based my faith in the love work I was doing. Together, each of us had grown and embraced openness. I knew it worked for me, but I also knew it worked for others; I saw the proof in our connection and in his changes. Our severance pulled the rug out from beneath my faith that the work I was doing was effective.

Finally, I had built up a reputation in the community as someone doing good work. How could I face people saying that I was working on this spiritual project; it used to be two people with a plan to grow. Now it is just me, and I need help. Am I willing to go forward when people I respect are urging me to stop?

In addition to the fear, there is shame at admitting that something I care deeply about isn't going well. How can I be as open as I've been when my openness can be used to hurt me? I'm hugely sad at what I've lost. I'm tired; I don't want to have to rebuild important parts of my life.

We're still breathing; I've begun to work with my chakras, energy swirling up and down through the core of my body. The music has fallen away; I'm falling into my own little world. I need to be there for a moment, but Susan and the thud of the flogger bring me back.

I am not alone. I stand firmly at my spiritual home, in the room where I met Venus, bound to a cross, vulnerable before my tribe. Yet in that vulnerability is strength. I've opened myself to grow, to change. I've opened myself to accept the fire of strength that is offered to me.

Susan has moved on, embracing my entire body with her work. I spend a few moments luxuriating in the physicality of the sensation. For the first time, I smell myself over the wood of the cross. I'm certainly not sexually excited; it's mostly fear and nervousness that I smell, although there is the core of my musk present, reminding me that I've embraced my primality, and that too is an aspect of myself I've accepted. I'm sure that opening again to smell is a change in me: I've been sweating all along. Now though, I'm able to connect with the physical.

The energy is building. Flogging has long since passed from purely sensual. She switches to the smaller flogger. There's some sting now. She's good: my entire body is her surface. She circles me; every part of me is invited to be physically present. Her control is excellent. I'm amazed that she can consistently flog my cock, something I'm comfortable with, avoiding my balls entirely, which is very important.

I can do this work. In fact, I am doing this work. I can connect with people anew: she's standing right in front of me, her sting on my belly, wrapping to my flanks. If I can find someone in mutual need, open to them this deeply, I can survive a lost connection.

I'm doing the work on another level. Together, I'm guiding someone through a new experience as they give me exactly what I need. I am teaching and practicing love. I'm relearning openness and connection with my feelings.

Yes! I can succeed in doing the work I set out to accomplish. It's time. I need the full power of the experience for what comes next. I say something to Susan. She hears, "Give me all you've got."

That's not quite how I intended it to come out. I certainly didn't want to challenge my top. She doesn't hear a challenge though: she hears my need for physical intensity.

She delivers. The sting focuses me in my body. I begin to cry. I give up being defined by my connections to others. I will not be validated by my reputation in the community. I will stand on my own strength, believing in myself. I still value connection, value receiving feedback on how I can improve, and take responsibility for my actions. However, I will stand strong and do the work I am called to do even if some believe I will not succeed.

I'm crying with relief but also fear. This is a different kind of fear though: I am releasing the crippling fear and lack of confidence. Now I face the familiar fear of a hard path and difficult growth ahead. I embrace my old friend: this fear will keep me sharp, drive me across the uncertainty ahead. It is a part of the journey.

Now, I am fully in the circle, in myself. Susan and I form a unit, her strokes anchoring me. We throw forward what we will discard into the circle. Together, with the power we have raised we send it on its way, mixing it back into the energy of the festival and greater world. It mixes and returns, rejoining the greater cycle.

We dance, giddy in the high of a scene and ritual well-done. We all come together and close.

Then there is time for after care. Susan and I talk, thanking each other. I honor what she's done: she too faced great vulnerability in bringing something this intense to someone new. I tell her some of what I experienced, some of what she did for me. It is time to embrace three true things: you are loved; you love; you are love.

After I go to the fire. It is my first fire of the season. There was a ritual here, but I have arrived after it has drifted to revel. That's good: it is the revel I need. Not even the no-fucking cold will hold me back. I step out of my clothes, divesting myself of shoes as I enter the circle. The drums and fire greet me as I begin to dance. I am home; I am in my tribe. We will grow and heal together. I have regained my course.

I am blessed. I think how surprised even the me of six years ago would be to hear this story. He was a computer programmer, sitting behind his keyboard like millions of others; he didn't have adventures like this. Of course, he was totally blind, so the computer talked and the screen was often dark. No one is normal when you get to know them close enough.

It all started when I took that small step, inspired by a tale of vulnerability and openness, much like this one. I came to this fire—to this exact fire circle. Perhaps I was standing right here when the consort called to Venus and she came.

Of course I'm still that computer programmer, and now I'm so much more. For you see he's always had the hurts, the pain of loss, the fear. Now, together, we have the strength, and opportunity to find healing and bounce back, better than ever.

Everyone has the opportunity to find their own path to adventure. It may not involve spirituality at all, or it may involve spirituality entirely different than mine. Or perhaps, next May, I'll meet them around this fire right here. Anyone can take that first step, follow their path, and before long, they will be their own blind programmer running alongside a pagan priest: the old intermingling with the new. Find a small way to be vulnerable and open, to grow. Follow it, and at each step choose for it to be right—choose to live in the best of all possible worlds.

A Nerd Was Awesome

When Lily said it, she watched James's face contour into a frown firstly of confusion then of some other emotion which she could not easily place. It was a plan that had been two years in the making, since the first time he had spoken to her in sophomore year and now barely two weeks to graduation and with the help of Susan, she had finally had the guts to say the words to him.

His lips opened and shut, struggling with an out-pour of words that never really made it out of his lips. Lily quickly looked at Susan for support. Susan was more sharp-eyed, one who seemed to impress her conviction on another without the unnecessary fuss of fear. With Susan, Lily thought it was either of two options. It was either James would agree to her request, a really simple one, of course, he was already in her apartment drinking alcohol and playing games with the girls since the early hours of the evening. Lily swallowed hard.

James's eyes never left her body. Hers did, distractedly, finding comfort in the little details scattered about in the nightshade of her apartment.

The bottle of alcohol, which was placed between the trio, was her most frequent fascination. Drunk halfway and the little shot glass by it like a lieutenant, Lily wondered if it has been necessary a move to convince James she liked him. Susan had said it would help. She had naively assumed it was to help with James but slowly and more certainly, the stains of tipsiness on her own being led her to an understanding of who it had been for. She had been a different person that evening and she loved it even though the confidence was nowhere near where she wanted it to be.

James turned from her for the first time since the revelation and looked to Susan for any signs of collusion between the girls. His handsome profile made Lily whisper a subdued purr.

His fine brown hair, stained with strips of more colorful gold always neatly cut even like his nails. His eyes were a dreamy black, one which allured and drew in attention when he demanded it. His nose was the perfect shape, not so aquiline and not so large. Lily knew she would kiss those lips of his for a long time if he let her. It had been two years and she had just asked.

He was a magazine model who had fallen out of the front cover by error, Lily thought to herself the many times she lay in her bed going through his features in her mind, refereeing the wrestling between temptation and confidence. Confidence had won this evening with some help from Susan's presence, but whether it had won James over was yet to be seen.

"Do you mean what you just said?" James asked, his right now jumped with the query.

Lily hesitated, looking to Susan and then back at James in a quick motion of her head's swing.

"Yup. She does," Susan answered, sighing and made the obscene gesture with her hands. "She just dared you to have sex with us. Now, your call!"

Lily could not tell if it was the confusion that made the boy all the more handsome, but she thought his face was paler as he waded his way through the thick pool of indecision towards the shore of a conclusion. It was a long haul but he pursed his lips. She knew his fingers had come upon the first sand of that shore.

"You ladies are beautiful but do you think I'm the one...?" His words dried up in his mouth and his shoulders dropped. Lily sensed he was having to doubt himself and she wondered if her hunch was true.

"Look, James. If you don't want to I'd understand," Lily muttered in easy resignation.

"No. No," James said, sharply. "I want to. I think it would be awesome. It has to be better than beating my meat to sleep like I do every other evening."

Lily's alarm met its match in Susan's face, but Susan's was more subtle. James shared the concern when he sensed he had spilled more information than was necessary.

"You don't have a girlfriend, James?" Lily asked, quivering but with more confidence than she had a few minutes ago.

"I don't think anyone would want to go out with me. They think I'm a nerd," James said, giggling.

"You're smart and that's OK." Lily swept her butt across the floor and towards him when Susan winked at her.

"I've always thought. Never mind." She canceled the thought.

"Are you a virgin?" Susan asked, complementing the end of Lily's speech.

"No. But I don't get sex often," James revealed without hesitation, and in truth.

"So you know what you have to do," Susan hinted, and snatched the bottle of alcohol from the floor and took a swig. "Hmm," she called with a grunt, passing the bottle to Lily who also drank and passed it to James.

James's hands trembled when he started to drink and Lily calmed him by putting her hands on him. She then took the nearly finished alcohol bottle and placing it back on the floor.

"Here, let me help you with that shirt," Lily said, moving astride his legs and sat on it.

She leaned towards him to kiss his warm lips, and the world in James's eyes faded to a cozy black.

They kissed intimately for minutes for an eternity, both basking in the pure delectation that their innocence with each other provided when Susan joined them when breaking up the lovemaking. She cupped James's head in her palm and culled him away from Lily and in her direction. James thought Susan's kiss was less warm than Lily's had been; being more direct towards the point of lustfulness which his boyish desires craved. With Lily, it was lovemaking. With Susan, it was fucking.

James's heart raced as he caressed Lily's butt as she sat on his hands, both legs about his sides and kissed Susan. He half expected the show to be over before they even got a chance to get it on, scarcely able to bring himself to the realization that it was him with both the girls engaging their passions. The sense of surrealism of the events hovered over proceedings even when Susan let his lips go. He returned to kissing Lily and pinching her ass closer and spreading them apart in a rhythmic stir.

He tapped her ass once and Lily giggled in his face. He opened his eyes just as she did hers as telepathy had communicated on both their senses. Her wide eyes from his position held something deeper than attraction and for a moment he thought it was just the alcohol clouding his sense of judgment, but the more he thought about it, the more it made sense. If she was not at least attracted to him, she would not have proposed such a dare.

He recalled some of the moments vaguely when she might have hinted towards his lure and he smiled as he pieced them. Lily placed her hands on his chest and withdrew from him, biting her lower lips seductively as she did.

"It's a beautiful thing to find love isn't it?" Susan teased and they both laughed. "I'm uninterested in that. Now, enough of that funny shit and let's find me some release."

Lily pushed her hands down James's body, picked the hem of his shirt and slipped it upwards by his shoulder, then above his head.

His bare chest was beautiful, even though she had had no expectations of his body, she was pleasantly surprised. His chest had been well exercised, the muscles on it already divided into two finely separate pieces. She ran her hands over it and her body shook from delight. Susan was out of her clothes and bra, wearing only her pants. Lily stood up to help herself out of her clothes and Susan replaced her on James's laps.

Susan did not kiss him. James had not expected to be kissed. It was something about her, a certain roughness that he was in to entertain. It was the thrill of unattached sex, she owned the vibration of the kind of girls that would fuck you tonight and not even say hello to you when you met them in class the next day. People like Susan were incredibly attractive for the sake of their coldness, male or female versions of them and with her on James's laps feeding her breasts into his lips, he understood why.

James placed one hand on Susan's back for support and the other on her chest to better direct her breasts into his mouth. His hand on her bare ass was a sensation he struggled with. He kissed her pink smallish nipples and sucked on them blindly even as Susan moaned, massaging then with both her hands until the mound was firm. It wasn't long before the nipples were erect and Lily returned to them.

Susan pushed James slightly and he fell on his back. Susan directed the exercise from her point above him, her body made into an obstacle that cast itself over the bleak light so that a halo was about her frame like a divine being. Her firm breasts and erect nipples called and James moved to answer when she stopped him with her body across his chest.

"Blow him," Susan said to Lily who quickly get to the task without delay, slipping his trousers off his waist as Susan fed him her nipples one last time. It was time for something else.

Lily gasped when she pulled James's pants to his ankles and returned to sampling his cock. It was easily one of the biggest she has ever seen, curvy and lengthy, the type that was sure to find sensations in a woman's body wherever it might be. Susan turned to her at the noise and when she too turned to see it, she laughed. Susan leaned back and stroked on it together with Lily, and when Lily put her lips on the penis, Susan left it to her.

For James, it was as though the several heavens of pleasure known to man had descended on Earth and it's manifestations to him was in Lily and Susan. Lily's mouth on his cock was the most pleasant feeling of all. Susan had already muffled his moaning when she had sat on his face, her shaved pussy in his mouth, feeding him all of it. She was as wet as a pool on a rainy day and he loved the smell of her juices as they made their way across his lips and some of it on his mustache. She smelt like tender flowers for all of the roughness which she exhibited, a steady pool of wetness. To imagine his cock in her pussy was not difficult to conjure as Lily gave the sensations as he would expect of her. Susan never took her pants off, James just pushed it aside as he tongue fucked her, slapping her thick ass and flicking his tongue about her clitoris.

"God damn," he cried, when Lily deep throated his cock, gagging on the meat and slurping with the same move. It was a difficult and clumsy maneuver to get Lily's face out of the way when she deep-throat on it again, summoning his ejaculation quickly. Perhaps she knew what she was doing for when his cock spasmed quickly and he started to shoot his load, she did not take her mouth off it, instead, she pressed her face against his crotch so that he shot the load against the back of her throat.

"Good Lord!" he blurted, breaking a sweat after the ejaculation.

"Ah ah, not so fast," Susan said, realizing what had happened and she moved away from his face down to his dick, switching places with Lily.

James's hips when numb for a few seconds when Susan licked on it, tingling the tip of his penis, where a stinging pleasurable sensation was most focused, to get the cum off it.

When Susan climbed his cock in a reverse cowgirl position, James knew. The sensation was tighter and wetter. He reached his hands and touched on her butt once before the activity escalated. Her butt muscles twitched as she sat atop his laps, his cock halfway into her, ready to slowly give satisfaction to the rod and herself. James sensed the twitch and before he could rub on it as his cognition instructed, Susan rode out of his hands. James dumbed his senses to the thrill and diverted his attention to pleasing Lily.

Lily, unlike Susan, was a screamer when she received pleasure and James gave loads of it with his tongue, lining the damp pussy with his tongue and licking the walls on the insides with such dedication that she creamed into his mouth whole screaming out her enjoyment, drowning the grunts of the other two in her presence.

Susan took her time sitting on the cock and fucking it halfway until she was creamy enough to lift herself into a squat, fucking the entire thing until James regained sensations on his lower region. She held both his legs to keep her balance as she threw her ass against his cock, bouncing her butt against his crotch and making a creamy mess of his cock and the root of his shaft.

Lily stumbled off James's face when she started to cum from his tongue work, vibrating unto her side as the waves of pure release hit her and screaming. James moved Susan off him and rolled on his side to pick himself up. He stopped on his knees and pulled Lily closer, shoving his face into her pussy and licking on it to intensify her pleasures, working at it until she could take no more, pushing him away.

He turned around, managing both their attention in short bursts as he grabbed Susan to himself so that her butt faced him. He grabbed one of her cheeks and smiled when he thought of how thick her ass was. He slapped her ass and squeezed the cheek, pushing

Susan's back so that it arched in the way that he wanted.

With one hand on her back and one hand on his cock, he eased himself into her from the back. As soon as he was all in, he placed the hands on her hips to keep her still, shortening the distance between each thrust. The image of a whitish paste on his cock incensed him sexually and he was in a frenzy when he started to whip, bounding and rebounding off her quickly as the whitish substance increased.

Susan held onto the floor as James fucked with the strength of an ancient deity of lecherousness. It had been years since she has been so fucked that she came, but James achieved that with his thrust upon the third minute of steady unbroken thrashing.

"I'm coming," she cried, bolting off his grip as she did. He followed her to the ground when she fell on her side, fucking her cum until her pussy from the force of the activity pushed his cock out as she gasped for oxygen.

Lily edged closer, recovered from her own ecstasy. She looked in his face and smiled, reaching her hand to his dangling cock and stroking it softly.

"You're something huh?" she said, still smiling.

James reciprocated with a smile and silence, with pride as a soldier that had vanquished them both in a war of pleasures. Lily was back for more and James was more than willing to oblige.

He held out his hands and she moved into it, as though he were a magnet and she was iron fillets. He held her head up and looked down into her eyes. The blank look on his face confused her and only when he smiled did she smile. He bent over her and kissed her as his fingers moved to her pussy, rubbing on her clitoris and scrubbing the strip of her pussy. He sensed she was wet and he stopped kissing her.

With both of them facing each other, James held Lily and rolled onto his side to the left. He held her right leg over his hip and lowered his body so that her left leg was beneath him without touching even as he lay.

"Aww. Would you look at the lovers!" Susan quipped mockingly at the pose which the couple assumed. Neither of them paid her any mind to save the smile of acknowledgment which they shared.

James slid into the tight pussy slowly and it purred, stuffed and stretched wide by his cock.

"Oh shit!" They both cried for different reasons. Lily's fingers on his back scratched a little as she tried to accommodate the full length of the cock which he pushed into her body.

James breathed through a grunt as he attempted to thrust, Lily lowering her body to meet him halfway in the exercise. It was unbelievably satisfying so that James had to throw his head backward to ease himself. Her pussy lubed his cock with a transparent coat and the thrusting became easier.

Lily's moaning was music, accompanying the sound of their slapping flesh against each other. If there was any doubt that Lily admired him, it was clear by the time Lily said those words at that moment.

"I love you, James," she said, wrapping her arms around his neck as he stroked, pushing her ass up for deeper penetration.

James was an easy man to please. The night had started slowly but surely it was ending with such a bang that even he could not have imagined it. He felt his toes curl and his legs go stiff as semen traveled the length of his shaft to the tip. He moved to pull out, but Lily held him to herself. A feeble attempt was put up to resist, however, it was too late.

James lay on his side, overpowered by the second cumming than he had been by the first. All he wanted to do when he was spent was shut his eyes and dream endlessly of the evening.

A special Weekend

Lynn and I had the most wonderful weekend recently. A friend of ours stopped over and we all had a night that we would never forget.

Isabella is a long-time friend of mine. She is short, voluptuous and very bi. She and I have flirted for ages and she always thought Lynn was cute as well. Over the years, they grew closer as friends and both commented on how pretty the other was (have I mentioned that Lynn was bi too?).

Well, Isabella called me up and said she wanted to come over and have some fun. I was definitely interested and a quick phone call on the cell confirmed that Lynn was looking forward to it as well.

Marie came over late in the evening and we sat around talking and relaxing in each other's company and friendship. We made converastion with Anne (our roommate) and her date for a while and Lynn went up to bed feeling suddenly tired. Isabella and I conversed longer with them to seem social as we stole feels of each other's body when nobody was looking. At one moment, I went to 'help her find something to drink' in the kitchen, which gave us the opportunity to kiss and fondle each other's bodies until we were breathless and determined to continue it upstairs.

She commented that she was Lynn's guest and was 'going to mess with her for going to bed early'. I decided I was going to take a shower because I wanted to be fresh and ready for whatever the night held. I squeezed and rubbed her ass down the hallway to our bedroom and opened it. Lynn laid beneath the blankets, but was definitely not asleep because she turned around, as Isabella climbed into bed with her, and started kissing Isabella. I took that as a positive sign, so I smiled at both women and stepped out for a very quick shower.

After my shower and when I went back into the hallway, I could hear soft liquid sounds and sighs from behind the door. I went into the dark room and turned the lights on to find both girls sitting on the bed. Lynn was naked behind Marie who was exposed from the waist up, her large breasts hung enticingly with erect nipples. They were smiling up at me as Lynn was kissing her neck and stroking her body.

My clothes were quickly shed (put on just in case the roomies were in the hall) and I smiled at Lynn before I kissed Isabella passionately on the lips. I felt her heat burn into my mouth before I moved down to her ample bosom and started sucking her breasts, nibbling and chewing on those large nipples. Isabella stroked my head. I noticed she still had her jeans on under the blanket, and of course, they had to go.

Marie understood where my hands were heading. She leaned into Lynn and lifted her hips to help me ease them off of her. After pulling her jeans off, I sidled up to Marie's left, putting her between Lynn and myself. As they went back to kissing and fondling each other, I feasted on her breasts, kissing up and down her side. My hands stroked up and down her thighs, then pulled them apart to expose her freshly-shaved pussy.

I lightly touched her there and felt her breath catch in anticipation, which fueled me to spread her wide open. She was so wet that her juices freely flowed from her, coating my fingers as they started circling and stroking her clit. Lynn slid down and worked her way down Isabella's body to suck on her other breast.

I moved down as well to get a better angle so I could slide a finger deep into Marie, whose groan was so deep and heart-felt that I knew she hadn't been touched that way in a very long time. Her body clenched my finger and her hips worked up and down to get every bit of feeling from that initial penetration.

I was at the bottom of the bed, licking her legs and pushing a second finger deep inside ... then I curled them and stroked her special spot; Marie's hips jumped off the bed and her eyes were as big as saucers when she gasped from pure pleasure. I looked at her through my long braids and said, "I told you that I learned some new tricks ..."

By this time, Lynn had come to the bottom of the bed as well and was kissing Isabella's thighs as my fingers were doing their magic. Inch by inch, her kisses went up from the knee, slowly and achingly working their way toward her wet, hot, dripping pussy. Lightning seemed to shoot through Isabella's body when her lips made contact with Marie's clit, Lynn's tongue was flicking and fluttering all over her sensitive button.

Combined with the thrusting, twisting and polyrhythmic motions of my fingers, she was constantly stimulated, never knowing how I was going to move next as I twisted deep inside her.

Marie started coming very hard, bouncing up and playing with her nipples while grabbing at Lynn's head. The wetness created by them poured over my probing fingers, soaking my entire hand which made my fingers move in and out of her nearly frictionless. Her G-spot was my target and I hit it with every finger flick, twist and combination that I could manage from that position, and she loved every second of the pleasure. Lynn excused herself to go to the bathroom and I slid down between her legs to press my tongue flat against her clit. I licked up and down her pussy, making a point to rub the entire raspy flat of my tongue against her clit. My fingers rubbed her pussy all over, spreading her lips apart and moving her juices from her clit down to her pretty, puckered asshole. Isabella moaned even louder at the contact and pushed against my probing hand.

Marie's fingers gripped my head, pulling me deeper to tongue every bit of her. Her thighs moved back and forth, alternating between clasping my face when she comes to spreading wide to give more access for my probing hand. Lynn returned to the room and watched us for a few moments while rubbing my shoulders, asking me how good the flavor was. My response was rather muffled by Isabella's thighs, but I gave an extra flick to Marie's G-Spot with my fingertips and made her come as punctuation to my statement. Lynn went up to Marie's side and they continued to kiss.

Marie turned to Lynn and started sucking her breasts, making Lynn press against her talented mouth and moan softly. I reached up between Lynn's legs with my other hand, spread her legs and eased a finger into her tight, wet hole. She sighed with pleasure as her liquid heat engulfed my finger while I worked my way deeper into her wetness. The unique pleasure of having fingers moving in and out of two women simultaneously can only be described best by experiencing it ... I became so erect that my shorts were tight and my cock was begging to be released.

I reveled in the incredible sensations I received from these two lovely women and received such incredible sensations from both at the same time: texture, reaction to penetration, the unique way they orgasm, the wetness caused by stroking their spots ...

I began pleasing both women at the same time, but in different ways and speeds. Lynn had a little to drink, which makes her extra-tight, so I used one finger inside her, pushing deep because she loves penetration and the occasionally rubbing of her G-spot. With Isabella, I had two fingers inside her super-wet pussy, twisting them inside of her like the twin serpents on a caduceus. I flicked her G-spot often, giving her a continual set of orgasms while she feasted upon Lynn's breasts and body.

Some time later, Isabella wanted to return the favor to Lynn and flipped over on the bed to dive, face-first, between her thighs. Isabella's tongue made contact almost immediately. Lynn's back arched and the first of many pleasure shocks rippled through her body.

I stood, watching the pleasure before me: Lynn's writhing body being devoured by a voracious Marie, who was feasting as though it was the first meal to a starving woman. Marie's big, round ass was up in the air, looking delicious and inviting. I was torn as to whether I should slide my super-hard cock inside her or play with her a bit longer. Lynn looked up at me and mouthed what I understood as 'Get her'.

I blew Lynn a kiss, which was lasciviuosly returned, then went down and kissed a wet trail down Isabella's back and over her big pretty ass. I massaged her round curves, knowing that she loved her ass being played with as much as I loved doing it. I spread her cheeks, then started licking her tight little hole with vigor. I put a hand on each cheek to keep her spread wide and pushed my tongue deep inside. She clenched my probing, twisting muscle and bucked up at my face to get even more inside her sensitive orifice.

I moved a hand down to rub her clit, driving her delirious with pleasure as she was making Lynn. My tongue went in and out of her over and over, stretching her slightly and getting her even wetter than before . Eventually, I pulled my tongue out of her ass and licked her pussy for a long time, feeling her juices all over my face. I slapped her ass intermittently to make her grind against my mouth.

Lynn was in a near-state of delirium from how Isabella was eating her. The slurps and sucks from between her legs meshed perfectly with the gasps and moans that came from her lips. She tried to pull away but Marie locked her arms around her thighs and held her down for a bit longer. Lynn, knowing she was at the mercy of a woman whose pleasuring would not be denied, fell back on the bed, fully enraptured by the delights of Marie's lips and tongue.

I eased a finger into Marie's wet, relaxed ass and two fingers into her even wetter pussy, pumping her with long deep strokes. Both of her tight holes milked my fingers as though they were my cock, and I could imagine how my swelled member would feel penetrating her luscious body. I was relishing the fantasy of filling her with my manhood so much that I was intensely throbbing and started to leak precum, causing a spot on my shorts to spread.

I was broken from my fantasizing by the very loud and strong orgasm she had. Marie's body clamped down hard on my fingers and she twirled her hips around, grinding against me to savor every moment. After catching her breath, Marie released my fingers from her grasp and Lynn from her hands, then slid up the bed to her. I watched them kiss and lick each other's faces, then I seized the opportunity to lick Lynn's open wet pussy, tonguing her up and down with gusto.

My hands held her hips down and kept her bucking down slightly so I could see over her sexy body. Both women were adoring each other's faces, necks and shoulders with kisses and licks. The sight of that passion made me even harder than before. I pressed against the bed with every movement on the mattress, causing achingly sweet vibrations through my shaft and balls.

I licked and sucked the sweet nectar from her body for so long that she got overly sensitive and started pulling away, but I had no intentions of letting go. Both women started pushing me away, and once the seal of my mouth on her clit was broken, she scooted back to catch her breath and calm down a little.

I moved up to where I was earlier, putting Marie right in the middle. Lynn and I began kissing her all over again, sucking her hard nipples, our teasing tongues against each other. Lynn and I reached between Marie's legs, getting our fingers wet all over again, then slid them inside her simultaneously. Our fingers pumped and twisted inside her at two completely different cadences until she came hard and shuddered.

As I moved up to kiss her again, my erection pressed into her thigh. She grasped it, then stroked it passionately, massaging my entire length. I looked into her eyes and calmly asked, 'Find something you like?'

She replied, 'Oh hells yea!' with a throaty giggle. I leaned over to kiss Lynn and she said, 'It was time to take care of me'.

Isabella told her to jump on me and ride, but Lynn told her she could go first, which surprised Marie and made her blush a little. Lynn excused herself to the bathroom again and I moved to the middle of the bed, legs spread with my manhood standing at full attention, eager with anticipation and curious as to what the rest of the night would have in store for us.

Isabella got between my legs, grasped my shaft and began sucking me so hard and hungrily that she had to be satisfying a long-wanted craving. Her hot, sucking mouth swallowed about half of me from the moment my swelled head passed her moist, hungry lips. I could feel her tongue slither up and down my manhood when she would pull me from her mouth then swirl over the head as she pulled me back in deep. She felt so good sucking and licking my cock that I nearly lost it. I had to throw my head back and moan loudly for some time; the sounds of my own pleasure combined with Isabella's wet, sucking mouth helped bring me back down from the clouds and help calm myself.

Lynn returned to the room and was greeted to see Marie's mouth stuffed full of my engorged cock, yet plenty still for her hand to play with. As she was sucking me deep, she started stroking me at the same time, rocking up and down as she pleasured my entire length. All the rocking made her ass point up in the air, inviting Lynn for some more foreplay.

Lynn looked up at me and we winked at each other before her face disappeared down between Isabella's cheeks. I know she must have been licking furiously because Isabella was moaning and groaning loudly, even with her mouth full of me. She reached below to rub the area below my balls, which made me pour more precum into her mouth; she sucked harder to make sure every drop was pulled into her hungry, gulping mouth.

After she decided she had to be filled, she sat up and Lynn was licking and kissing her back and neck. I sat up and kissed her breasts, squeezing them until she moaned. I put my arms about her and pulled her down on top of me so she could straddle my body and get ready for me. After she put the condom on, she got up on top and started to line herself up to slide down my shaft .

The look of bliss on her face when my head eased inside her was beautiful. We both moaned deeply at the heat when I started to enter. Lynn watched from the foot of the bed, seeing Isabella slide farther down on me. The initial look of bliss turned into the sexiest look. When she pushed down, impaling herself with my shaft, I must have gotten in much farther than she expected because her eyes slid into the back of her head and her mouth opened wide in pleasure as my entire length inside her. That image of pure eroticism will forever be burned into my mind.

Soon Marie started moving up and down on me, faster and faster, gripping me from root to tip. I had to think of something—anything—other than how good she felt or I wasn't going to last but a minute more. I held her hips and told her to grind on me so she could feel me pulse deep inside her. She was loving the twisting actions of our bodies being so close—pelvis grinding to pelvis—then I started to flex my cock inside her, thickening the shaft, enlarging my head and making it twitch back and forth, pressed all the way inside her. That feeling caused her to make the sexy moan for me again. I knew she was enjoying herself, so I sat back and enjoyed the ride.

Marie started bouncing, twisting and turning so happily on my shaft. I squeezed her breasts and tugged her nipples every time I could to send shocks down to her clit. We started thrusting harder and harder, faster and faster until she came so massively that she jumped up from me and just stood there, shivering and shuddering from the power of her climax. Lynn and I held onto her for a few moments while the shaking stopped and she laid back on the bed with us.

After she'd calmed down a bit, she told Lynn to climb aboard me. Lynn straddled me and was about to ease down, but I stopped her and told Isabella to put my cock inside Lynn. She loves to watch and the thought of getting to penetrate Lynn with my cock was too delicious to pass up. She gave me a Cheshire Cat smile, grabbed my shaft from the root, then put my head right against her wet opening, then pushed us against each other until I popped inside. She stayed right between our legs, watching happily at the sight of my shaft disappearing and reappearing into Lynn's dripping wet pussy.

I felt Isabella's hands on my legs and I asked if she was enjoying the show. She was devouring every movement with her eyes, moaning softly in agreement as she watched Lynn's sinuous motions while she rode me. I decided to spice things up a touch and told Lynn to turn around so her back was facing me and she could lean back on my chest. Lynn started turning around, keeping me inside her as she bounced up and down.

When she had completely turned around with her back facing me, I helped her ease down so her back lay against my chest. This exposed her to Marie, who got to see Lynn's pussy up close; her hard, throbbing clit and lips spread wide open with my thick, hard cock stuffed deep into her tight hole. Marie crawled closer and sucked on Lynn's clit, which made her come instantly. Lynn's juices flowed even more freely over me and she had a string of multiple orgasms without pause.

Marie's hands proved to be as agile as her mouth. Her fingers start playing over Lynn's spread lips and my balls while she continued to suck and lick Lynn senseless. Isabella grabbed the exposed part of my shaft, working it up and down to increase the sensation. I played with Lynn's upper body as Marie pleasured below. I kissed and nibbled on her neck as I played with her breasts, squeezing her breasts hard the way she loves it, and used that as leverage to push her body even deeper on my shaft. Between Marie's mouth and my cock, Lynn came so hard and squeezed me so tightly that I popped out! Marie noticed with surprise that Lynn's orgasm was so intense that she had squeezed the condom right off me!

After Lynn climbed off, Isabella got on all fours and started kissing her again. I got behind Isabella and rubbed my head against her wet slit that parted her lips then thrust deep inside. Burying half of my shaft inside her with the first push, she groaned and pushed back against me to fully sheathe myself inside her hot, slippery body. Her hips moved up and down so forcefully that my manhood felt as though it was on a rollercoaster. She asked—no, demanded—that I fuck her hard, so I grabbed her hips and started thrusting deep and hard into her. I slapped her ass and thrust deep, flexing and swelling my cock so hard that she cried out in pleasure.

Lynn lay beside us kissing Isabella and playing with her large, swaying breasts. I massaged and slapped her large, round cheeks to the coos of her delight. My only goal at that moment was to give her every bit of pleasure she wanted, what she deserved and what she desired. I kept up my pounding and thrusting until she collapsed on the bed, shuddering uncontrollably in pleasure. Lynn pulled Marie's head to her bosom and caressed her as she pulled off out my cock and panted over and over, grinning about how much she was overstimulated.

My manhood—thick, swollen, pulsing and glistening—stood above the women with a drive to pleasure and be pleasured. Lynn lay back with open legs and beckoned for me to come closer. I nestled between her thighs and leaned back to give Marie the view of me as I slowly slid my entire length inside Lynn's hot, wet pussy. Her back arched and I could feel her every inner muscle stretch to accomodate my thrusting. We groaned and hissed when I fully sheathed myself inside her hungry, twisting body. I leaned forward and put an arm around both women to pull them together so we could all have a hot, threeway kiss. Our lips and tongues met and we all moaned as we tasted and savored the flavors on our mouths, which got us even hotter from the thrillingly unique contact.

Nearly breathless from the kiss, we all leaned back for a moment. Lynn looked at me, begging me to give it to her hard and deep. With renewed resolve, I pinned her to the bed, fully in control and thrust inside her with long, twisting strokes. Lynn mewed at me, completely enraptured by my forcefulness and threw her pelvis at me with every deep stroke, sucking me even deeper into her tight wetness. Marie stroked my arm as she murmured words of encouragement.

"Fuck her good ... give it all to her ... make her come hard ... fuck her harder, harder, harder! Yes baby, it looks so good watching you fuck her like that ... I love watching you two fuck ..."

Lynn's hot, tight, wet body wriggled around my cock, combined with Marie's hot body pressing up against us, and soon it became too hot for me to handle. Amidst the sounds of Lynn's orgasms, Marie's erotic words and the slick liquid sounds of our bodies moving against each other, I pulled my manhood from Lynn's body. Blast after blast of my seed flew from my cock, arcing over her body as though it were launched from a cannon. I gasped uncontrollably and had to brace myself against the wall for support while my orgasm ripped through my entire being.

I purred like a great cat and smiled down at the incredible women before me. I was even more pleased and surprised when they began feeding drops of my seed to each other with their fingertips, smiling and winking at me the entire time. With my composure somewhat regained, I leaned down to kiss both women and told them how much I enjoyed myself.

Isabella said that it was better than she imagined it would be. We'd been together a long time before and she knew I'd be incredible, but she was so surprised at how good Lynn was in bed. We looked at Lynn to ask her how she enjoyed it, but all she could do was smile and giggle. I held both women against me in a very loving embrace, kissed them both and simultaneously wished for the moment to never end, hoping the next time would be even better.

A Satisfied Smile

She had him right where she wanted him.

Charlotte had never felt so accomplished her whole life. And she was yet to get started with the plan she'd laid out, so there were more feelings of accomplishment where that came from. She had always known there was a way to beat a bully without using her fists, but could never have thought this would work with her beast of a husband. She'd been married to Sandler for three years. He hadn't been a beast from the start and has been nothing short of a Romeo. But she realized just now narcissistic the man truly was. All he cared about was himself. She had put up with all his bullshit for so long.

It was time to show him that roles could switch.

And there was no better day to get back at him than on a chilly Sunday morning. As usual, the man had returned home in a drunken mess. She knew without a doubt that he'd been to his favorite club and had probably wasted some hard-earned cash on a whore or two. His drunkenness has made it all too easy for her to strip him naked and restrain him to the bed. Now here she was, sitting at her dressing table with her eyes fixated on him. The man, motionless as a log, lay supine on their king-sized bed. His chest rose and fell as he breathed, but that was as far as his movements went.

Charlotte glanced up at the wall clock. It was a few minutes past eight in the morning. She'd thought he would be up by now. She decided to give him a few more minutes to round up his sleep.

And then, just as though he'd read her thoughts, he stirred. She straightened her spine, a smile darting across her face.

"Wakey wakey," she said in a sing-song voice.

Sandler's eyes fluttered open. He groaned, his lips parting to let out a yawn. His hands twitched in an apparent attempt to cup his mouth, but they stayed fixed on the bed. His eyes widening with obvious confusion, he moved his hands again. This time, he tried to move his legs as well, but they didn't budge.

He stood no chance against the thick ropes she had restrained him with. The loops were strong enough to withstand his beastly tendencies, so when he started to growl and struggle, his hands and legs flailing on the bed as he tried to break free, so it didn't come as a surprise to Charlotte. She would only be surprised if he didn't put up a show like this.

"You know," she said, "struggling like this will only cause the ropes to bite into your skin."

"Untie me," he ordered. "Or I swear I will—"

"Oh, darling, you will do nothing at all, believe me. If there's anyone who is in a position to give orders right now, it certainly isn't you." She rose from her chair, the six heels of her stiletto-heeled shoes perforating the transitory silence following her words.

Sandler was about to speak again, but at the sight of her, he could only gape. She was dressed in white thigh-high stockings and a garter belt, her breasts hiding in a lacy white bra. She found it intriguing how Sandler was clearly upset, but his body seemed to have a mind of its own. His cock leaped to life at the sight of her, preparing itself to push through her tight pussy.

"Hot, aren't I?" She winked at him.

She'd never dressed so sensually for him, so he probably never thought she had it in her. She advanced toward him, her hips swaying with each step. Locks of wavy blonde hair settled on her chest, hiding her cleavage.

She whipped her hair back, her eyes aglow with lust. "Sleep well, darling?"

She waited for a response, and when it didn't come, she chuckled. She didn't need his response anyway.

"I take that as a yes." She mounted the bed and started crawling between his legs. She leaned toward him, her breasts barely an inch away from his cock. She lowered her head some more, and then she breathed through her mouth, letting her steamy breath tickle his torso.

While she crawled her way toward his face, she could feel him trembling beneath her. And when his stomach clenched hard, she couldn't hold back a laugh. She dropped her ass, making a chair out of Sandler's torso.

Sandler groaned, his Adam's apple bobbing as he swallowed hard.

Charlotte's lips found his left ear, and then she whispered, "There's a camera, Sandler."

Sandler bristled.

She laughed. "Dear husband, you see that, over there?"

Without turning around she pointed at an alarm clock on the dressing table. "That's a spy camera, darling."

"No!" Sandler shook his head, disbelieving.

Charlotte chuckled. "Yes, darling."

Once again, Sandler tried to break free from the restraints, but his action yielded no results. It only had him rubbing against Charlotte's pussy. She bit her lower lip to suppress a moan as his skin rubbed her through her crotchless panties. She could feel her pussy juice pooling beneath her. She glided back and forth, smearing Sandler's stomach with the natural lube.

"Now," she said, "here's what happens. You have to submit yourself to me, darling, and do whatever I request of you. Else, this video goes viral and everyone, including your silly little bitches, will see you tied up and powerless, while I humiliate you for the silly excuse of a man that you are."

"No you won't," he said.

"That's what you think?" She giggled. "You are so, so funny when you wanna be, Sandler. I mean, this is you trying to be funny, isn't it?"

She didn't wait for him to respond. "Has to be! I mean, you don't expect me to sign the divorce papers and walk away without giving you a memory to last a lifetime? Or do you?"

"What do you want, Charlotte?"

Charlotte grinned. She loved the tremor in his voice when he spoke with so much rage. She could almost see the fume escaping his ears.

"I wanna give you a memory to remember when we go our separate ways, Sandler," she said. "Please let me know if I have to say this again."

Sandler groaned.

Charlotte slipped back again, and then forward, making his skin sleek with her juices. "You love it when

I do this, huh? When I smear my pussy juice all over you like some high-end lotion?"

She glided back once again, bumping so hard into his cock that he jumped from the impact.

Sandler groaned harder. "Oh, God."

"There is no God, darling," she said. "Only you and I. Oh, and Sergio."

"Sergio?" he asked.

"Well, say hello." She reached back to grab his cock, and then she squeezed.

He let out a voiceless scream. She laughed, watching his dark mouth as his lips flew open. She didn't hear the door open or shut, but when Sandler gazed behind her with a horrified face, she knew they were not alone anymore.

Sergio was here.

"What did you think?" She made a face, feigning surprise. "That I was all dressed up for you?"

She clicked her tongue and shook her head, her lips stretching into a smile.

"No way, darling," she said. "I only entertain real men. Men like you with five-inch cocks deserve none of that. They're useful though, to clean me up after I've been fucked so bad. I wonder how I put up with you and your lack for so long. But I'm done now, because darling, I've had enough of your petite cock to last a lifetime."

She squeezed his cock again. From his clenching jaw, she could tell he was gritting his teeth, trying hard not to be vocal.

"What now?" she teased, letting go of his cock. "You won't cry anymore? Is it because of Sergio? Shy now, are…"

She trailed off as Sergio's palm found her back. His palm glided down toward her ass, and then he snaked his arm around her hips. She turned sideways to kiss him, an exaggerated moan escaping her when he squeezed her breasts. Sergio was stark naked, his huge cock ready to plunge deep inside her. She wrapped the fingers of her left hand around his shaft, gently stroking him while he kissed her.

She broke the kiss and nibbled her lower lip. "Oh fuck! Here's a real man. A real fucking man…"

She looked up into Sergio's baby blue eyes, a smile breaking out on her face as she found him grinning. They'd never met before, and she'd only found him on Tinder, but she'd seen from his nude photos that he had a monster between his legs.

"Mmh!" she hummed.

She licked her lips and turned toward Sandler who had suddenly turned speechless. With her left hand still wrapped around Sergio's cock, she pointed at it with her right index finger and gave it a rather vigorous shake.

"You see this right here?" she asked. "This is a real cock. I'd say it is eight inches…"

"Nine, actually," Sergio corrected. He buried his face in her neck and started to smother her with kisses.

She tilted her head sideways to accommodate his lips on her neck. "Nine fucking inches right here!"

She heaved a sigh as he unhooked her bra, and then she giggled as he buried his face between her breasts, flicking his tongue around them while he slipped his hand between her swollen pussy lips. Sergio rose to his feet and grabbed his cock, aiming it at her face like a gun. From where she sat, she could give him a blowjob without having to adjust her position. The thought of giving the endowed man a blowjob while she pinned Sandler down with her weight was too juicy not to entertain. She grabbed Sergio's cock once again. His girth pushed her fingers apart. He had apparently gotten thicker and longer in the few seconds she'd let go.

She brought her lips to his cock, and just as the thick head met her lower lip, she turned toward Sandler. "What now? You didn't actually think I was going to fuck you, did you?"

All smiles, she turned toward Sergio and took him in her mouth. He tore her lips apart and sank deep inside of her, past her teeth. She moved her head back and forth, setting the pace, even though his hand rested on her head. She soon picked up the pace, sucking him nice and fast. Spittle gathered in her mouth and sought to escape through the corners. She let them. They tickled down her mouth, spilled onto his cock, making her lips glide effortlessly.

His moaning voice was music to her ears, urging her to go even faster. Her hair danced back and forth, tickling her bare skin. Sergio grabbed her hair with both hands and pinned the golden locks to her head. He moaned loudly, his gruff voice rough against her eardrums.

Charlotte shut her eyes so all she could stare into was a sea of black. This way, there was no sight in the way of her pleasure. Beneath her, she could feel Sandler squirming. Was this Sandler trying to get some of the pleasure? She could have sworn he was rocking his body in an attempt to rub her pussy. Maybe he actually was, and it intensified her pleasure. She moaned, a wave of adrenaline stealing over her. Her eyes squinted open and she glanced at Sandler. She winked at him and returned her attention to the huge cock she was sucking.

Sergio stabbed his way toward her throat. She didn't object. She held his cock in place and didn't back away when the gag reflex came knocking for the first time.

With him deep inside her mouth though, choking her with his huge cock, it was impossible to breathe.

The second gag reflex, much more overwhelming than the first, had her pulling away from him. She took him in her mouth again, this time, she wrapped her fingers around the base of his cock. She looked up at him, holding his gaze as she sucked him. Sergio was breathing hard, his chest rising and falling. She didn't need to place a hand on his chest to know just how fast his heart was thumping. She could see from his flaring nose that he, just like her, had to give in to an overpowering surge of adrenaline, letting it flood his insides.

"Fuck, Bri! I'm gonna cum!" he groaned, his cock pulsating inside her. "Want me to cum all over him, eh?"

Charlotte smiled, considering Sergio's idea. "He's all yours then."

She chuckled, her eyes fixed on Sergio as he pulled out of her and mounted the bed to stick his cock inside Sandler's mouth. Sandler clamped his mouth shut and flung his head to the side.

"Come on now," Charlotte said. "Be good! Well, as I said, if you're good I'll keep this little porn clip to myself, but if you're not…"

She smiled, watching Sandler's lower lip reluctantly fall open. She'd known he would comply. He wouldn't want his porn video circulating the Internet. She bit her lower lip to trap in a bubble of laughter as Sergio stroked himself just above Sandler's face. And then, with a growl, Sergio rained down cum on Sandler's face, marking him like the shameless sissy that he was. Globs of cum dropped into Sandler's mouth.

"You know better than to spit that out!" Charlotte said, stopping him from spitting.

He made a face and gulped it down. More drops of cum rained down on Sandler's face, and when it was all over, Sergio shook off the rest of his cum.

Charlotte sat on Sandler's torso the whole time, watching him swallow. "You're quite a swallower. Good job."

"Please," he begged. "Make this stop. Just tell me what you want, Charlotte."

"To see you submit yourself like a loyal dog." She leaned toward his face and whispered, "By the way, do you know this song with the lyrics 'bottoms up'?"

Once the last phrase rolled off her tongue, she stuck out her ass and buried her face in the crook of Sandler's neck. She grabbed her left ass cheek with her left hand and moved it sideways, away from the other ass cheek. Her fingers slipped through her ass crack to tease her dripping wet pussy. The groaning bed told her of Sergio's presence behind her. She bit down on her lower lip, awaiting the stab of his cock. She stiffened as his huge cock kissed her asshole, and then he slipped past the tight hole, finding warmth between her pussy lips.

She cried out. "Yes, oh fuck! Deeper, please!"

She grabbed Sandler's shoulders and squeezed tight. She moaned and cried as Sergio reached deeper, and although her voice was too loud for Sandler's comfort, she made no attempt to adjust her pitch.

"Fuck, Sergio! You're a man! You're a real fucking man!" she gasped, trying to catch her breath. "Oh yes, harder!"

"Love it when I fuck you so hard, huh?" Sergio asked, his voice shaky as he pounded harder.

"Yes, yes, yes! I fucking love it! Oh Sergio, you feel great inside me. So fucking great!"

Her pussy sloshed and clenched, her ass rocking back and forth. Sergio grabbed her hips, and then he slammed so hard, she collapsed on Sandler.

Sandler groaned from the impact.

"Damn it Sergio!" Charlotte cried. "You are so good! So fucking good!"

She hummed, and then she clamped her lips together. In the absence of words, she kept humming, deep moans erupting from her clenching stomach.

"Oh fuck it feels so good when you fuck my pussy like that!" she cried. "Sergio…"

"Mmmh baby?"

"Cum inside me…"

She reached for Sandler's neck and wrapped her fingers around it. Her fingers tightened around his throat, only easing up when she felt him stiffen, two veins stretching down his forehead as he tried to breathe. She let go of his neck and he gasped for breath, his nose flaring.

"Oh fuck!" Sergio cried out. "Here it comes!"

He thrust harder, deeper, faster. And then, he growled, emptying himself.

Charlotte stuck out her ass some more, thrusting back to pin herself to Sergio's body. He was sweaty despite the air condition in the room. She was just as sweaty, her body gliding along with Sandler's as she thrust back and forth.

Sergio pulled out of her, his hands gripping her waist. He reached down and planted a kiss on her ass.

"You're so full of me, baby," he said, spanking her ass.

"Time for someone to get to work," Charlotte said with a smile. "Untie him, Sergio. Let's see if he has learned the ABC of submission."

She heaved herself off Sandler and lay on her back. She parted her legs as she watched Sergio untie Sandler.

The man would probably say no, refusing to lick her clean, but for his sake, she hoped he wouldn't.

Once untied, he got on all fours, his eyes finding the raw flesh between her legs.

He dove between her legs with a speed she hadn't seen coming. She gasped, knocked out of breath, but she quickly found her breath again. As though her legs weren't already parted, Sandler flung them further apart and buried his head between them. She whimpered at the first feel of his tongue on her sensitive skin, but she made no attempt to move away. She watched, her eyes gleaming with pleasure as he sucked her like a thirsty man who had just found a bottle of water after a lifetime in a desert.

Fuck the divorce, Sandler, she thought. I should tame you instead.

She smirked, loving the sound of that. Prior to now, she had never thought of taking the reins of their marriage. Now though, after having a taste of what it felt like to be the one in control, with so much power at her disposal, she concluded that this was just how it was meant to be. It was only a matter of time before her narcissist of a husband became a proper sissy, living to serve her.

With a satisfied smile, she parted her lips, letting Sergio fill her mouth with his cock once again.

Relationship Is Much Harder

Olivia woke up as the sun rose early in the morning. She yawned as she sat up in her bed, stretching her arms. Today was the day, it had to be right? She swung her legs over the edge and got to her feet. She walked over to her mirror and looked at her reflection. 5'3, petite but big breasted with long brown hair. She was naturally gorgeous, yet she'd never been with anyone before. She had grown up in a fairly strict religious household, so she had never dared to bring anyone home, lest they feel her father's wrath. But now it was different, she had moved out a year ago and was living on her own. She had her own apartment, her own job, and her own life. Nobody could tell her what to do anymore.

She'd gone through puberty like any other girl, her hormones flowed through her body. She'd done a little experimenting with herself and masturbation with whatever privacy she could get. Yet something deep inside her burned for something else, she wanted…no, she needed to have a man inside her. She picked up her phone from her charger and downloaded the tinder app.

Hopefully someone will be willing to sleep with me, she thought to herself as she set up a profile.

It didn't take more than a couple of minutes before she had matched with a handful of guys. She had some casual back and forth chats with people before being blunt and telling them she was a virgin. She settled on a nice looking Caucasian male named James. He had brown hair, a muscular physique, and was tall. They messaged back and forth for a while before setting a time and a date to meet up.

Okay, see you then, she texted him as she turned off her phone.

Olivia gave out a huge sigh of relief. That hadn't been nearly as bad as she had imagined. She felt bad for people who were actually looking for a relationship, surely that was much harder.

She took off her nightgown and turned on her shower, placing a hand under the running water to wait for it to get up to a proper temperature. As she stepped underneath the water she closed her eyes and imagined James running his hands all over her body. She cupped her breasts with both of her hands and moaned as she massaged them, pinching her nipples slightly as she did. She wanted to be perfect for tonight, so she washed her hair thoroughly and scrubbed every inch of her body twice. She shaved perfectly making sure she was smooth everywhere, including the most important area, then turned off the shower.

As she dried herself off she looked in the mirror. She wasn't bad looking was she? Hopefully he didn't think so. She didn't have much experience with dating or standards of appearance.

She put her hair up to dry and patted herself down as she walked to her closet. She picked out a pretty red dress she'd been saving from her senior year in high school. She'd never gotten to wear it, but at least she had it. She laughed quietly to herself.

Picking out a matching pair of lace boyshorts, she pulled them on and set them on her hips. She looked at the pretty red dress. She could have dressed more casual, but he'd invited her to a pretty upscale hotel in the city. Maybe she was under-dressing for the occasion. She was pretty sure he wouldn't complain at all.

Olivia pulled the dress up her slender body and zipped it up in the back. She did some light makeup before taking a deep breath. Now came the real question, flats or heels? She hesitated for a second before deciding on a pair of red heels she'd bought to match the dress. With one final check she was ready to go. She got her keys, hopped in her car, and drove to the hotel.

As soon as she pulled in front of the hotel her eyes went wide with admiration. It was far more marvelous than anything she had anticipated. The structure was at least twenty stories tall and adorned in large glass windows all the way up to its sides. She got out of her car and handed her keys to the valet who stared at her awe.

"Pretty amazing isn't it?" he said as he got in her car.

"Yeah, it's really something else. I didn't even know stuff like this existed," she replied as the valet drove off.

She walked up the steps to where a greeter opened the door for her. "Thank you," she said and smiled warmly.

"Have a good evening madam," he said, then smiled back, motioning her through. She walked up the front desk and patiently waited for the receptionist.

A handsome man spoke up. "Good evening miss, do you have a reservation here?"

"Yes, my last name is Lawrence, the first name is Olivia. I'm supposed to be meeting someone named James Rogers here tonight," she replied.

"Ah yes, he checked in a few minutes ago. Here's a copy of your room key," he said as he handed her a key card. "You'll be up in room 503."

Olivia smiled and took the card. "Thank you for your help."

She walked over to the elevators and pressed the button for Floor 5. She waited patiently until the ding signaled the elevator and the doors opened for her. As she got into the elevator and pressed button 5. She shifted nervously, smoothing out her dress one last time. The elevator stopped on the fifth floor and she walked down the hallway, stopping at the designated room. She took a deep breath and slid her key card in.

The lock clicked and she turned the handle to enter the room. Looking out the window was who she assumed was Jason, he turned around to face her and smiled. He looked exactly like his profile pictures. Tall, clean-cut, muscular, and very…very handsome. Despite being quite attractive herself she instantly felt insecure about her looks.

"You're gorgeous," he said. "I'm almost speechless."

Olivia blushed at the compliment and replied meekly, "You're not bad looking yourself."

"Thanks," he replied.

There was an awkward silence for a few seconds before James spoke up. "Are you really a virgin? There's no way with someone as pretty as you."

Olivia wasn't sure whether to take that as a compliment or an insult and replied somewhat taken aback. "Excuse me? What's that supposed to mean?"

James stumbled with his words realizing how that came across, "Oh, I just meant that you're so gorgeous, you could have any man you wanted. I'm just kind of surprised that you've never been with anyone at all. The personal reason, or religious, or...?"

"Ah well, I'm flattered. I grew up in a pretty strict family so I never had the chance. Now I'm out in the real world by myself so...here we are," she said and smiled shyly.

James smiled back and there were another few seconds of awkward silence between the two. James finally took the initiative and stepped in towards Olivia, placing both of his hands on her hips. He looked down at her soft blue eyes and leaned in for a kiss. Olivia looked up at him and gently pecked him on the lips. They leaned their foreheads against each other and smiled. She wrapped both of her arms around his neck and he placed an arm around her lower back. He gently cradled the back of her head with his other arm and pulled her in close for another kiss. The two of them locked lips passionately and kissed each other deeply. They tilted their heads slightly and James moved his hand down from Olivia's lower back and gave her ass a slight squeeze.

Olivia smiled into her kiss and moved both of her arms to James's shirt. She slowly unbuttoned the top one and worked her way down until it was open down the middle. She pulled it down his arms, revealing his well-toned body. James reached behind her and gently pinched the zipper between his fingers and slowly started pulling it down, making sure to read Olivia's response as he did. She started to breathe a little faster but he assured her with, "It'll be okay."

He unzipped it to the end, stopping at her waist, then stepped back. She let the dress fall down her waist and onto the ground, revealing her petite waist but ample DD cups. She blushed red and covered her breasts with an arm out of habit. "You're perfect. I've never seen someone so beautiful in my life," he said.

Olivia couldn't think of anything to say. After a second she responded, "You don't have to lie to me."

James unzipped his pants and let them drop to the floor before stepping out of them. "I'm not lying, otherwise I wouldn't be getting undressed for you right now."

He moved over to her and positioned himself behind her. He placed both of his hands on her hips and pulled her close, she could feel the bulge in his boxers pressing against her lower back. He kissed her on the neck warmly and she moaned as a shiver ran through her spine. She looked up at him and both kissed again from over her shoulder. He moved his hands from her waist up to her breasts. Olivia reluctantly moved her arm away from covering them, letting them drop free.

James cupped both of her full breasts one in each hand and firmly massaged them. Olivia placed her hands over his and moaned at the sensations running through her body. The feeling was so foreign to her, but one thing was for certain, it felt amazing. He pinched her nipples with his hands softly and she squeaked. James stopped for a second to make sure she was okay.

"No, don't stop, I just didn't realize how...*sensitive* I'd be," she cooed softly.

James continued massaging her breasts for a minute before moving his right hand down her abdomen and to her panties. He traced his index finger along the inner seam of the waistband playfully, then pulled it back out. Without much warning, he fully cupped her mound with his right hand and gave a firm squeeze. Olivia's knees instantly crossed as a warm sensation ran through her pelvic region and into her pussy.

"How does that feel?" he whispered in her ear.

"It...it's amazing," she said.

He cupped her mound firmly and used his middle and ring finger to massage the outside of her opening, creating pressure against it. Olivia moaned quietly, blushing as she did, but unable to control herself at the sensations running throughout her body. James moved his hand to the waistline of her panties again and pulled them down, revealing her smooth, virgin pussy. She blushed again as no man had ever seen her fully exposed, but he again comforted her. "You're the best catch I've ever had."

This made her feel safe and she grabbed both of her breasts fully with both her hands. She started to massage them herself James used his two fingers to trace lines along her outer lips.

He moved his hand slowly to her clit then gently touched it with his middle finger, sending a pulse throughout her entire body. She moaned loudly and grabbed her breasts. He gently massaged her clit in small circles with his middle finger for a few seconds, making her moan in pleasure. He kissed her neck and nibbled gently on it as he did so, slowly moving faster and faster.

Olivia began to feel pressure building behind her pelvis as the familiar feeling of orgasm approached. "D...don't stop," she whimpered. James kept rubbing her clit as she squeaked, "Ah, ah, ah."

Her breaths became faster and more shallow until an orgasm crashed into her body and her legs buckled from under her. James used his strong physique to help hold her body up as wave after wave of pleasure slammed into her. Her pussy muscles contracted as James relentlessly massaged her swollen clit, causing her to gasp. Eventually he slowed down and so did her breathing. He pushed his two fingers inside her for a brief second and spread her juices around her outer lips.

He turned her to face him and picked her up gently in his arms. She wrapped her legs around his waist and her arms around his neck as he carried her to the bed. He laid her down on the bed, her juices dripping from her soaking wet pussy. He climbed on top of her and kissed her neck softly. He kissed down her body, moving from her neck to her collar. He licked her right nipple with his tongue, then took it in his mouth and sucked softly. He used the right hand to play with her left breast as he rolled her nipple around between his fingers with one hand and his tongue with the other.

Olivia moaned happily as small ripples of pleasure shot through her chest down to her waist and back up to her brain. He kissed down her stomach to her v-line and licked a long line up both sides. He moved down once more to her tight pussy and licked her clit directly, making her squirm. He placed both hands on her thighs and went down on her, licking her clit softly at first, but quickly picking up his pace. He thirstily drank up her juices, licking from near her anus all the way up to her clit.

He took her clit in his mouth and sucked gently, tracing small circles around her pearl with his tongue. She moaned loudly as he used a free hand to stick his middle finger inside her. He navigated his middle finger around her insides, feeling the walls of her soft folds then stuck his ring finger in as well. He made a 'come hither' motion with his two fingers and pulled on her g-spot. Olivia's eyes rolled back in her head as he massaged her g-spot with his hand and her clit with his tongue. He started to move faster and faster as her clit and the pressure behind her g-spot began to swell.

"W…wait," she cried as she felt herself about to cum. She placed her hand on his head and went to push him off of herself, but he gripped her thighs firmly and held her down as he continued to stimulate her sensitive parts. "I…I'm going to cum…"

Her words were cut off by her orgasming again, squirting juices onto the bed and into James's mouth. She blushed bright red and began to apologize as he slowly moved off of her, licking his lips. "I'm sorry I tried to…"

He held a finger to her lips and moved his body on top of hers. He pecked her on the lips and then slid his boxers off, revealing an adequate 6 or so inch cock. He placed it against her opening and Olivia began to breathe fast again. He rubbed it against her outer lips, lubricating his tip before pressing against her opening. He started to push inside slowly, moving his cock in and out. He pushed a little bit deeper each time until his tip entered her fully. Olivia gasped as he pushed himself further inside her. She moaned as her virgin pussy gripped his cock tightly.

"You feel so good," he grunted as he started to thrust in and out of her. She wrapped her arms around his neck and pulled him close as he thrust in and out of her, building up his pace quickly. Before long he was pounding her tight pussy as she moaned with each thrust. Pressure started to build up behind James' pelvic wall and his balls began to contract. Olivia could feel his cock growing stiff as she also neared another orgasm.

She let out one last loud moan as her pussy contracted, a powerful orgasm hit her for the last time. James's cock throbbed and spasmed as he shot a huge load of cum deep inside her virgin pussy. He shot load after a load of cum in her before he took a deep breath. Both James and Olivia breathed heavily as they came down from their orgasms. He slowly pulled his cock out, letting his cum drip out of Olivia's tight hole. She smiled as she got up, the cum dripping down her inner thighs.

"I hope that wasn't too disappointing for your first time," James said.

"It's the best I've ever had." Olivia winked.

Printed in Dunstable, United Kingdom